LIGHT & SHADOW

THE WATCHER SERIES SHORTS AND EXTRAS

ROBIN WOODS

Epic Books Publishing

Lead Editor: Beth Braithwaite
Additional Editing: Brooke E. Wayne

Cover Design by Robin Woods
Slayer Tattoo and French Coven Coat of Arms Illustrations by Vera Walker
Historic art from Wiki Commons—a source for public domain media.
Poetry by Shakespeare and Browning are public domain works.
All rights reserved.

Summary: An engaging series of short stories, alternate perspectives, deleted material, poems, artwork, and scenes written to answer fan questions.

[Fiction-Young Adult, Fiction-Urban Fantasy, Fiction-Paranormal Romance, Fiction-Vampire, Fiction-Vampires]

Paperback ISBN: 9781941077214

CONTENTS

ARTWORK

FOREWORD

When I began writing the first novel in the *Watcher Series*, it was 1996 and I had just called off my wedding (only six weeks before it happened—but don't worry, I found my Prince Charming four years later). Consequently, I was in this weird emotional state. Writing became my refuge. I didn't write the whole book then, but I did write several scenes, picked a lot of the character names, and laid out the blueprint for my novel. It was a place for me to retreat.

I was teaching English for high school juniors and chose to make my protagonist that age. Since she didn't have tons of life experience to draw on, I used the literature I was teaching in my class for my character to use too.

Two years prior to this, I had graduated with my degree in English, so mythology and literature were fresh on my mind. Works like *Paradise Lost, The Book of Enoch, Dracula,* and *The Tempest* kept me company in the quiet hours. I also had a friend introduce me to the old, cult classic film, *Highlander*

(Thanks, Brooke). This, combined with *The Book of Enoch*, sparked my ideas for my Watchers. (No, it wasn't *Buffy*. This was before the show ever aired. But we did use a lot of the same source material.)

In late 2008, I went back to what I had written again and toyed around for a long time. But it wasn't until a student saw my manuscript sitting on a table and asked if she could read it that things got real. I nervously let her, dying a little bit inside. Then, she did the most magical thing—she asked if she could take it home to finish reading. It spurred me on, and I have never looked back.

The series is still a refuge, and recently, going back to it was like going home. Is it weird that the characters are so real to me?

Anyway, thanks for being a fan. This is for you.

(If you are still sitting there wondering which scenes I wrote in 1996, they are: coffee shop rescue, locker slut, apartment attack, caged, and blink yes or no. Plus, there are a first two chapters that will never, ever be seen. Like *ever*.)

Doubt that the stars are fire;
Doubt that the sun doth move;
Doubt truth to be a liar;
But never doubt I love.

—Shakespeare

THE SLAYER TATTOO

All Slayers have a tattoo somewhere on their bodies. Gabriel sports his on his left forearm, Uriel on her right shoulder blade, and Kez on his entire back.

Here are the translations for the Latin phrases.

Vitae—life

Veritas—truth

Aeternitatis—eternity

Dignatio—honor

Custodite proxima et future—take care of (or guard) the past things and future things

WATCHER HIERARCHICAL STRUCTURE

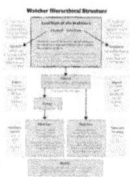

A friend of mine, who is a very visual person, asked me to sketch out how the Concilium works. Therefore, I give you the flow of power within the Concilium.

Additionally, you can see who belongs to each side.

Watcher Hierarchical Structure

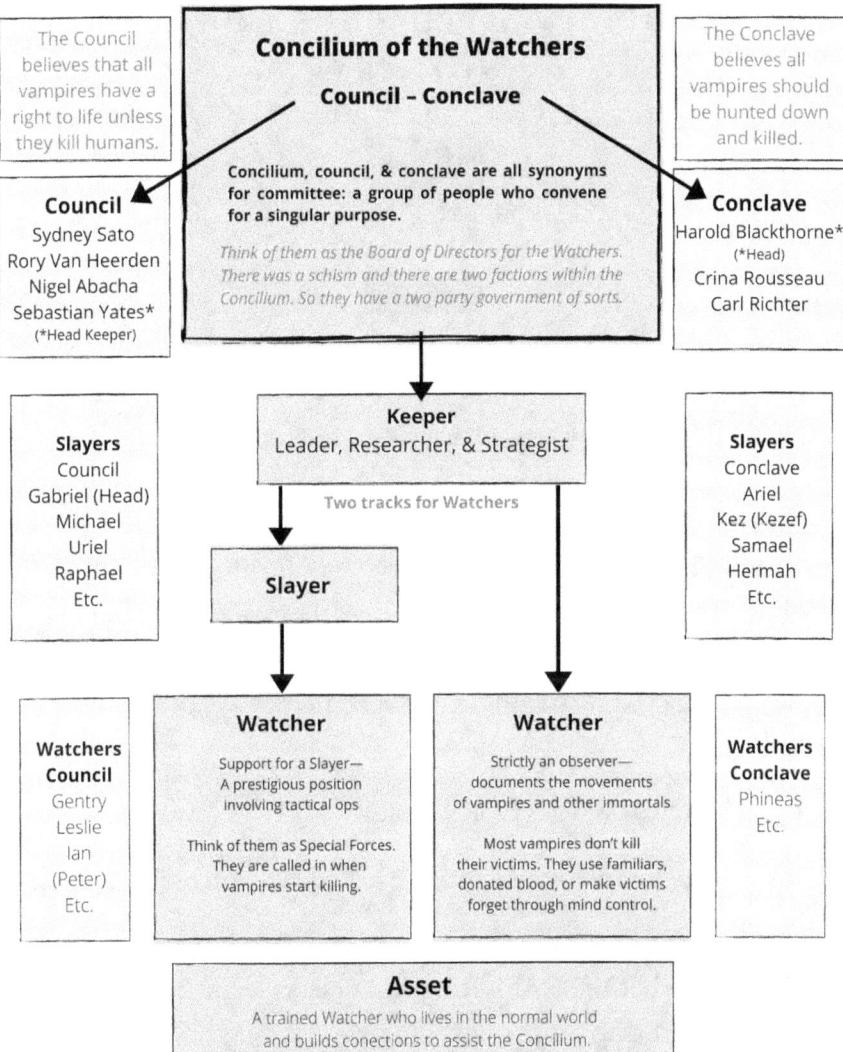

The Council believes that all vampires have a right to life unless they kill humans.

Concilium of the Watchers

Council – Conclave

The Conclave believes all vampires should be hunted down and killed.

Concilium, council, & conclave are all synonyms for committee: a group of people who convene for a singular purpose.

Think of them as the Board of Directors for the Watchers. There was a schism and there are two factions within the Concilium. So they have a two party government of sorts.

Council
Sydney Sato
Rory Van Heerden
Nigel Abacha
Sebastian Yates*
(*Head Keeper)

Conclave
Harold Blackthorne*
(*Head)
Crina Rousseau
Carl Richter

Keeper
Leader, Researcher, & Strategist

Slayers
Council
Gabriel (Head)
Michael
Uriel
Raphael
Etc.

Slayers
Conclave
Ariel
Kez (Kezef)
Samael
Hermah
Etc.

Two tracks for Watchers

Slayer

Watchers
Council
Gentry
Leslie
Ian
(Peter)
Etc.

Watcher

Support for a Slayer—
A prestigious position involving tactical ops

Think of them as Special Forces. They are called in when vampires start killing.

Watcher

Strictly an observer—
documents the movements of vampires and other immortals

Most vampires don't kill their victims. They use familiars, donated blood, or make victims forget through mind control.

Watchers
Conclave
Phineas
Etc.

Asset
A trained Watcher who lives in the normal world and builds conections to assist the Concilium.

THE ORIGINAL PROLOGUE FROM THE UNINTENDED

259 BC, Northern Europe, Celtic-held territory

"Staying here any longer is lunacy," he murmured, as a bitter wind clawed at them. "You pushed them too far," he said, looking over the balcony. Hundreds of torches snaked down the hillside towards the castle, a blaze of color in the midnight.

"I will handle this," she replied coldly.

"It's all a game to you, isn't it?" he asked, his voice tinged with disappointment.

"Isn't that what life is? Plotting a course, calculating the risks, and maneuvering for the advantage?"

When the epiphany hit, agony seized him. He stood in silence for a few long moments, his shoulders heavy with his revelation. "*I* have only been a game to you—an obligation."

She looked startled and tore her eyes away from the approaching crowd. "No, of course not," she insisted, as she turned and ran her fingers through his long blond hair before affectionately resting them on his chest.

He gripped her wrists, removed her hands firmly, and placed them at her sides. "Don't lie to me. I can read you too well."

"Belenus, I was born to be your wife."

"Well phrased, always the politician."

"This is what I was raised to be," she pouted, her calm a little shaken.

He let out a humorless chuckle. "That's right. You are the victim of your upbringing. You never embraced it."

The noise of the mob finally reached them and started to bounce off the stone walls. They listened as the crowd reached the outer gate. The iron clattered and groaned from the pounding.

He turned to her and said, "We should go."

"I'm not going anywhere—the guard will quell them."

"Even the guard cannot withstand this, vampires or not. You will sacrifice them for nothing."

"It is their job to die for me."

"*Please* come with me."

"Leave if you wish. I will not begrudge you."

He turned to depart, but stopped at the door. He placed his hand on both sides of the frame and leaned there for a moment. He spoke with his back to her. "I loved you, you know."

"I know," she replied softly, with some tenderness in her tone, though she did not reciprocate the sentiment.

He closed his eyes, choking back bile, knowing that everything he had believed about her was false. "Goodbye," he whispered hoarsely, aware they would be his last words to her.

Within seconds, he traversed the passageways to the hidden entrance of the catacombs. He slid aside the seemingly immovable stone with ease, lit a torch, and stepped into the blackness. As he replaced the stone, he heard the horrific clamor of the inner gate giving way, the splintering of wood, and the cries of pain. With sadness, he disappeared, never looking back.

DARKNESS—A HAIKU

A POEM ABOUT TYRAN

You are a dark thing
twisted, bent, and craving more.
Waiting to devour.

—Robin Woods

BOWEN: INTOLERABLE

HAS BOWEN ALWAYS RESENTED HIS BROTHER?

A Bowen & Tyran Reunion

Europe, 1664

BOWEN'S POINT OF VIEW

Bowen sighed. "Why have you come here, Brother?"

"You neglected to say farewell," Tyran replied flatly.

"It has been well over a year. Why now?" Bowen inquired, though clearly not surprised to see his kin.

Tyran pursed his lips and sat on the balcony overlooking the city street. Black smoke puffed from the oil lamps lining the cobblestone lane. The few people brave enough to venture into the streets were drunkards heading home or ladies of ill-repute selling their wares.

"And how is *Maman* (Mother)?" Bowen finally asked, after the silence had stretched into the darkness.

Tyran grinned over at Bowen, "Intolerable. As always." Tyran stretched his long legs out in front of him. "But what could you really expect? Her favorite son slipped out in the middle of the night without a word."

"I am not her favorite, and I *did* warn both of you I would leave."

"She never believed it."

"Mother should know better than to doubt me," Bowen replied shaking his head.

Tyran's voice softened uncharacteristically. "I have missed you, Brother." He paused and drew in a breath. "But you seem to be doing well." Tyran hitched his thumb over his shoulder towards the apartment and the beautiful woman sleeping inside.

Bowen squeezed his eyes shut and rasped, "Do not *even* consider it."

The smirk returned to Tyran's face as he chided, "You never share—always too attached to your food."

"She is more than food to me, and you know it."

"They always are. Too bad; she looks delectable—another fair-haired beauty." Tyran looked through the window thoughtfully for a moment. "How long will you stay with her?"

"What concern is it of yours?" Bowen inquired, his voice calm.

"So hostile," Tyran laughed as he stood up. "Now I certainly must have a taste."

Instantly, Bowen was standing before Tyran, blocking his path to the apartment. "Leave her be, and you can stay." There was a hint of defeat in his tone.

Tyran returned to his seat with a triumphant expression.

"Do not look so happy. You would not like her anyway. She is good."

"Then why are you going to break her heart? Or will you turn her?"

Bowen's shoulders slumped, and he plopped next to his brother. The real answer: he was lonely. He swallowed hard and replied, "You know my feelings on turning humans. I will make sure she has everything she needs when I go. She will be better for having had me in her life a brief time."

"So you will slink away into the night, as you did to your own family?"

Bowen cringed. "No. She's human and can have no hope of my return. I won't have her wait for me needlessly. I won't be cruel." He paused and indicated some soldiers loitering outside a brothel at the end of the street. "War is brewing. It is always convenient for *our* kind."

"Hides our kills," Tyran responded.

"Not that. Let's us disappear. I will simply need a uniform and a letter with a military seal to notify her of my glorious demise in the name of God and country."

"I see you have already thought through the details," Tyran commented, looking a little smug.

Bowen sighed again. "And to answer your question earlier. No, I do not love her. Though I do feel genuine affection."

"Then why the need to give her closure?"

Bowen closed his eyes and pinched the bridge of his nose. "When we were gods, Taranis, you were one of thunder and destruction. Your followers feared you. They burned men alive in the most horrific of sacrifices to appease you. Those wicker man rituals," Bowen's voice trailed, still hearing the screeches of pain and the smell of burning flesh as his brother looked on without a speck of empathy. "I do not—" he stopped short, realizing any judgments he had were useless. "Let us simply say that it is my last act of goodness before allowing you to drag me into your world once again."

"You say that as if you never enjoyed being worshipped."

Bowen stood and moved towards the apartment. "I do not claim to be anything better than I am."

"You would have fallen in love with her. It is who you are."

"No. I am done with loving humans," Bowen replied, resigned. "The spare bed has clean linens. The shutters are reinforced and will keep out the sunlight. She knows not to open them."

"You will not regret letting me stay," Tyran stated in earnest.

Bowen smiled sadly. "Good to see you, Brother." When he entered the apartment, he knew he *would* regret his brother's entry back into his life. Bowen wondered how many years it would take for him to be free.

IGNITED BY YOU—A POEM

Your love is warmth like
the rays of a thousand suns
powering each glance;
The heat of a raging fire
fueling each delicate kiss.

—Robin Woods

GEORGE: FIRST SIGHT

WHAT DID ROSEMOND'S MOTHER SAY TO GEORGE?

Allure Alternate Section for Chapter 2

GEORGE'S POINT OF VIEW

Despite silently grumbling my way here, I was delighted when I met my charge's mother, the immediateness of her warmth and humor drew me in. She was striking for her age and held herself with an elegant grace few could. Small wrinkles around the eyes betrayed years of both joy and worry. When she teased me straightaway, I understood my father's affection for her. I prayed that the daughter would be pleasant—and homely. If she had her mother's beauty, it would be distracting. I needed to focus and return home.

At that moment, the younger likeness of Helen Le Clair appeared in the doorway. All thought seemed to halt. I blinked. *Damn it all.* She was the most beautiful thing I had ever seen.

I squared my shoulders, feeling as if I didn't know how to hold my body, suddenly a schoolboy again. It took me longer than it should to wrangle my expression from awestruck boy into something professional.

She broke the initial eye contact, a faint blush spreading across her cheeks, and stared distractedly at something on the floor. When she returned her gaze, lavender eyes, pale like aquamarine, stared back at me. The initial shyness seemed to melt away as a subtle grin changed her expression. I was staring, but couldn't look away.

"Rosemond, this is Mr. Yates. He will be your escort."

The spell broken, I stepped forward, extending my hand. "Miss Le Clair, pleased to meet you."

"You're British," she said in surprise.

I wasn't sure what to say to this. Everything that came to mind either sounded petty or condescending. In an effort to avoid both, I turned to Mrs. Le Clair. "Zach and Sariel should arrive at any moment."

"A Slayer," she repeated, a question mingled in the statement.

To clarify, I turned back to my new charge. "They are both Slayers." When her expression didn't change, I realized the nickname, Zach, might be throwing her; it wasn't exactly an angelic name. "Zachriel."

"Ah," she nodded, seemingly satisfied, and turned away. She went to look out the drawing room window just as a vehicle idled up and parked behind mine.

Mrs. Le Clair lowered her voice, "The two suitcases there. I packed light in case you need to move quickly."

"Thank you," I responded setting off for the bags, the darkening landscape reason enough to set urgency in my pace. I picked them up in stride as I moved towards the motorcar; Zach and Sariel met me in the middle, both alert.

Sariel spoke, "Nice to see you, George. Can we be on the road within five? We are exposed here."

"I have her belongings; we can away in two."

Zach pivoted in the direction of the house. "I'll get the mother's bags stowed. I'll head north no more than a few minutes afterwards."

That urgency nagged at me again. I circled past them, loaded the bags, and headed back to the house. Mother and daughter were wrapped in a tight embrace, the mother whispering fervently to the daughter. The pain caused by their parting made me pause, wanting to give them a little more time. At the same time, empathy swelled inside me, not wanting to consider how it would feel having to separate from family forever.

It was getting dangerously dark, and I had to cut this short. I cleared my throat. "My apologies, but we really need to be leaving. The sun has already set."

"Mother," the daughter choked.

"I know, sweetheart. Now *go*."

I held the door open, and Miss Le Clair slipped past me smelling of rose and lilac.

Mrs. Le Clair took my hand, and I gave her my full attention, but she froze staring into my eyes. She was there, yet not there. After an elongated moment, she seemed to examine the features on my face and settled into some sort of knowledge. When her daughter stepped back about the interrupt, Mrs. Le Clair sent her out the front door with a look.

Then, she turned that icy gaze on me. "Mr. Yates, this assignment is going to take longer than you think." She sighed and shut the door, blocking her daughter from the conversation. "You take care of her. You have a good heart. I see that, please—" she cut herself off, swallowed hard and started again. "Don't let your guard down. I see information being exchanged. A traitor. Gunfire. Black eyes. Yellow eyes. A wedding ring. Someone from your past who you *can* trust. There are too many fragments to unravel here. But I do know that your life will not play out as you planned. Both you and my daughter are important; what you set in motion will change generations. And the danger is imminent." She sagged. "I wish I didn't have to burden you in such a way. There is no time. Rosemond is strong, but she has been raised in isolation. Please protect her." She placed her hand on the side of my face, startling me. The gesture intimate and motherly and more expressive than words.

My father had told me she was the real deal. I needed more information. "Who can I trust in the Watchers?"

"Sariel. I can vouch for no others. Go. My fate awaits me. Save her. Save yourself. Go now."

I strode out the door, down the steps, and past Miss Le Clair, keeping my back towards her, and took a few breaths trying to still myself.

At that moment, gunshots inside the house spurred me back into action. The Slayers were already running towards the house. Rosemond took breath to yell, but I managed to clamp my hand over her mouth to silence her with only a muffled "M." She was still struggling towards the house, so I looped my arm around her waist, half-dragging her backwards. She stomped on my foot and elbowed me before I had a chance to utter a word.

"It's me," I whispered, biting back the pain.

Instantly, she stopped struggling, but still tried to run to her mother. I grabbed her wrist, spinning her to my side like an aggressive Tango move, holding her to my side. Then glared at her to stay with me.

We both looked at the house. Zach had disappeared inside, the doorframe smeared with his blood. Sara almost inside, pointed at us and then at the motorcar and mouthed the word, "Go!"

I turned, placing my body between the house and Rosemond, starting to push her towards the Studebaker. Three more shots rang into the night and something that felt like a burning ember struck my right shoulder from the back and went clean through. Refusing to admit what the source of the pain was, I kept moving.

With her hand in mine, I sprinted towards the vehicle with her in tow, wrenching the passenger door open and dragging us both inside. Engine roaring and foot on the gas petal, we sped into the night.

All the while, her mother's words haunting me, "What you set in motion will change generations." *We would have to survive first.* Feeling the bullet wound in my shoulder and shock setting in, I held the steering wheel in a vice-like grip and simply prayed to make it through the night.

ONLY YOU—A POEM

Tumbling forward,
Into emotions only you could reach.

Glimpses of you…
Days of you…

My universe—
Forever altered.

—Robin Woods

ROSEMOND: REEMERGENCE

WHAT DID JOSHUA AND ALI'S GREAT-GRANDMOTHER, ROSEMOND, DISCUSS ON THEIR WALKS IN THE GARDEN?

After *Allure* and Before *The Unintended*

Southern Oregon

ROSEMOND'S POINT OF VIEW

Growing old was dreadful. I sighed and rocked my chair as I looked out at the gardens, watching as the heat rose from the soil in small waves like a hallucination. The heat felt good, easing the aches and pains in my body. My eyes drifted to my hands, which had once been so beautiful, and now betrayed my age. Absently, I rubbed at the dark spots as if they would smudge away. A breeze wafted over the back porch, ruffling the wisps loosed from my upswept hair and carrying smells that stirred memories.

Rollicking laughter broke out from inside the house, and a slow smile spread across my face. Having my family here for my birthday, though it wasn't my real one, made my chest tighten with emotion. I'd turned ninety-eight exactly one month ago. My husband and I would have had a secret celebration somewhere, like we'd had for his birthday—paying homage to who we were before we had to give up our names and birthdays time and again. Curse him for passing before me. He'd gifted me with a life of peace I had not thought possible. A tear streaked down my cheek and was immediately dabbed away.

I started rocking again, realizing I had stopped with the memories of my last night with—I stopped myself. Noise from within the house drew my attention, so I peered over my shoulder through the window. My granddaughter and her husband had brought up their neighbors this time, Amanda and Eric. They were best friends, and I had always adored them; the house certainly felt right brimming with people— with life. Their son, Joshua, had my great-grandson, Cameron, over his shoulder, and was galloping around the room. My great-granddaughter, Aleria, was taking advantage, tickling her brother with each pass.

Having Aleria here was like looking in a mirror at me from so long ago. I turned away from the happy commotion and looked back to the gardens. Both my daughter and granddaughter had escaped without inheriting my gifts. But when my great-granddaughter's eyes had grown lavender, I worried. Thankfully, I had not yet seen any of the signs; many of the Lux hadn't until they were a little older. There was a deep gnawing in me, wondering if I should have been training her...but I hadn't had a vision in many, many years. Maybe the power in my veins had run dry along with my descendants. I desperately hoped so—for their protection.

A bird squawking from its hiding place delivered me from my musings. The temperature was already dying down, and the shadows were growing deeper, although little time had passed. I wasn't sure why I was struggling with sadness. Almost a century of life spread out, filled with stories I could never share with any of them. Silence their only protection. A familiar feeling crept up my tired spine and settled into my ancient bones. I could not help but have my thoughts settle on George.

I glanced back inside the house for a moment at Joshua. Suddenly, the resemblance was utterly obvious. Remove George's British reserve and place him in this century, and you would have the beautiful boy in my living room. Joshua was a little taller and narrower, but the overall impression was the same. The dark wavy hair and thick lashes surrounding soulful eyes. There was a simmering strength in him.

Easing forward in the rocking chair, I carefully stood to my feet holding the rail tightly as I moved towards the steps, wanting to get away from the bittersweet memories that were threatening to overtake me. I was startled to find Joshua standing in the doorway. Glancing away, I wiped my cheek surreptitiously once more, then looked back at him, smiling as best I could.

"I was wondering if you were ready for our turn in the garden?" Joshua asked pleasantly. His eyes lingered on my cheek a split-second too long to have missed my tears.

I cleared my throat. "I would be delighted, Mr. Copeland."

He offered his arm. I looped my left arm through his and held onto his elbow with my free hand as we traversed the steps. We walked in silence for several minutes.

"You are a sweet boy for indulging me this way," I complimented, patting his elbow and looking ahead. I glanced up at him when I felt his eyes on me.

He regarded me with earnest. "I enjoy our walks." Then he shrugged. "I'm a teenager. I know how to disappear if I don't want to do something. Of course, you can't tell my parents that."

"It is in the vault," I replied, tapping my temple lightly. His candor was refreshing.

Joshua smirked, and then his face grew thoughtful. "How did you end up in Oregon? Your accent...you say some things like a New Englander."

"I do?" I asked, feigning ignorance, realizing I'd become careless in my old age.

"You pointed out some herbs using the 'h' sound. If you were from the West Coast, the 'h' would be silent."

"That's astute of you."

Joshua shrugged again. "You know how you can tell if someone is from Southern California as opposed to Northern?"

"No," I smiled.

"The freeways. Someone from SoCal will say, 'I'm going to take *the* 101.' NorCal will say, 'I'm going to take 101.' SoCals always add a 'the.'" He paused. "So, you didn't answer me. How did you end up in Oregon?"

I took a deep breath, contemplating what to say for a moment. Wondering how much of the truth I could divulge. Faking my death and changing my identity a dozen times while being pursued by evil wouldn't suffice. "There was a boy. Or maybe I should say boys. And some trouble. And I moved west to get away."

He furrowed his brow. "Trouble..." He chewed on the word for a moment, and then seemed to choose his words carefully. "Like scandal?" He paused, "It was easy to have your reputation ruined back then, wasn't it?"

I smiled at the fact he had picked up on the trouble being scandalous. "Yes. Divorce, pregnancies, and broken engagements could ruin a person when I was young. The world was...different, but inherently the same."

"What do you mean?"

"We may have traded horses for motorcars and telegraphs for cell phones, but the desire for power never changes."

"You remember those things? Telegraphs and horses?" Joshua asked hesitantly.

"I don't suppose there would be a more exciting time to live. I've watched the world transform before me. We had money, so I don't recall being without a motorcar, but I remember them sharing the road with horses when I was a small child. Not in the cities, but in the country. We had neighbors that had a moving company. They could move whole houses with their team of horses. You would be astounded by what people could do even without modern technology."

"I can hardly imagine it. I thought living without a microwave was rough."

I chuckled. "We had a country home with no electricity. We cooked like people did for centuries—over the fire."

A moment later, a sensation I hadn't had in years began at the crown of my head—feeling like icy fingers creeping through my hair and pressing into my scalp. I gasped and tried to press forward to the bench that lay not too far ahead.

In the past, I'd learned to control my visions and kept myself from losing consciousness, but I was out of practice. And this one was no normal vision. I was vaguely aware that Joshua had spun in front of me and was holding my upper arms.

My knees gave out, and the last thing I saw was Joshua's terrified face. At my age, he must have thought I was going to die in his arms, but this was my seer blood taking control.

Suddenly, I was driving a large truck and having a hard time staying on the road. My vision was blurred, and I glanced at my lap. There was an open bottle of whisky; I...no...he snatched it up and took a large swig, half of it spilling down his chin. Tears were plummeting down his cheeks. He felt utterly lost. I saw what he was going to do. He was on Highway 1 and was going to end it. Drive through the guardrail not far from here and plunge into the ocean. As he swerved around a hairpin curve, the bottle dumped onto the floor, and as he started to reach for it, headlights washed through the front windshield. The moment the truck smashed into the small sedan, I saw Amanda and Eric's faces locked in horror.

I was thrown to a new location in my vision. I opened my eyes and could see red and blue light flashing through the closed blinds. I sat up and peered through the slats. Police cars were lined in front of Eric and Amanda's house. My heart started hammering. I looked around the room and realized I was in my great-granddaughter, Aleria. She slid out of bed and trotted down the hall to her parents' room. "Mom...Dad...I think something's wrong. Police are out in front of the Copelands' house."

Anne, my granddaughter, sat up abruptly and rushed towards the front door as she shrugged into her bathrobe with her husband, Connor, on her heels. Before they could reach the door, there was a knock. Aleria hung back in the hall, watching her parents open the door. There were two uniformed police. The one in the lead was holding what Aleria recognized as Amanda's sparkly, blue cell phone. He cleared his throat, "Mr. and Mrs. Hayes?"

"Yes?" Connor replied.

"Do you know where I can find Joshua Copeland, son of Eric and Amanda Copeland? There was no answer on his cell phone." The officer held up the phone.

My granddaughter's voice was hoarse. "It's late back East. He is away at school in Philadelphia—Penn State."

"You were both listed on her phone under 'In Case of Emergency.' I am afraid there has been an accident. Do you—"

"Are they okay?" Anne interrupted.

He hesitated. "We really need to speak with their son."

Aleria slid down the wall and landed on the floor. Tears started to well up, and her throat became choked. She felt it. They were both dead. Silent sobs started convulsing throughout her entire body as she tried to keep silent and not draw attention. When she tuned back into the conversation, she heard her mother's words coming out in a sob, "...*both* of them?"

Darkness filtered over my vision yet again as I felt anger and hurt so deep it crept through my veins like a disease. I was a man, holding someone in his arms. A shiver ran through me. I wasn't in a man, I was in a *vampire*. I could taste her blood as he gulped it down greedily, wanting to make her pay, and not for something she had done but to satiate something else. She cried out for help, and he felt amused. He hadn't bothered to glamour her; he didn't plan on letting her live that long. He was purposely being reckless. Why?

The silhouette of a young man stumbled into view in the mouth of the alley. He was answering the girl's cry for help, and I felt myself cry out when I recognized Joshua. His bravery would end him.

It was apparent that the vision was coming to an end, but I was torn from the scene in the alley to one last location. I was inside another man...he was strong. Worry was swirling in his gut, although he kept his body relaxed as he drove his vehicle down a dark, country road. I caught a glimpse of the tattoo on the inside of his left forearm, and I recognized it instantly—he was a Slayer. He sighed. "Are you going to tell me what happened?"

There was silence. I desperately wanted him to turn his head.

"I came so close to hurting her," the voice rasped.

Protectiveness unfurled inside the Slayer, layered with a thick, emotional edge. He cared deeply for whomever they were speaking about, but he didn't utter a word. He was drawing out the other speaker with silence.

"She wasn't herself. She wouldn't have pushed me like that if she'd been. I know that." There was deep sorrow in his familiar voice.

"She needs you now. More than ever. It is time for you to return the favor. The weight of finding out what she is could destroy some people." He finally glanced at the passenger. Joshua—it was *Joshua*, and it was readily apparent that he wasn't human. He'd survived, but at what cost? And why would he be in the company of a *Slayer*? Additionally, this Slayer felt a kinship with Joshua.

"I would give my life for Ali if it would save her. She's all I have."

The Slayer let out a slow breath. "Retrieving the documents will take a couple of days. Get your head straight; when we return, be there for her. We did not show her all of the translations we completed. When she learns to control the power within her, she can change *everything*." An image of Aleria shivering in the rain rose in his mind, and of him wrapping a towel around her and giving her comfort. I liked this Slayer, he was different.

Joshua broke into his musing. "Gabriel, I—"

"You are in the prophecy, too."

"I-I am?" Joshua questioned in shock.

"I do not know that much now, but it is unmistakably you."

"How could some prophet from thousands of years ago know about *me?*"

"It mentions a potential mate of the Nexus who was 'orphaned' and 'turned by darkness yet follows the path of angels.'"

Joshua sighed, and fell silent for a long moment. "Gabriel, I want to—"

I tried to hang onto the vision for just a moment longer, but failed.

My eyes fluttered open as the vision receded. I realized I was propped against Joshua on the same bench I had been trying to hurry to before, though my aged body hadn't allowed me to walk to quickly enough. Joshua must have carried me the rest of the way.

"Oh, thank God," Joshua gasped. I believed he'd been literally praying.

A wry grin quirked up my lip. "Not dead yet."

His chuckle was choked with emotion. "I thought—"

I raised my hand and cupped his worried face. I shouldn't have touched him so casually, but he reminded me so much of George at this moment. "My dear, sweet boy. I still have a couple of years left in this body. I can feel it." The fears on his face seemed to ease. I dropped my hand to my lap and drew in a deep breath.

"Do you want me to help you back to the house? Should you rest?" he asked.

There was a tremor in my voice, "I promise you, I am not ill. I have…" I looked him straight in the eyes as I continued, "gifts, and I have been terribly, terribly wrong."

"I don't understand."

"Not too long from now, you are going to go through great tragedy. I wish I could do something to help you avoid it. I *need* you to be strong. There will be more than one calamity to befall you."

The afternoon sun illuminated his eyes, making them look like emeralds. Joshua's doubt was apparent, but he continued to listen.

"Aleria is special." I wiped a tear that decided to betray me. "I was *so* wrong. I should have done so much for her already. She will be in your life after the darkness has settled. Hang onto your history, to your humanity. You will need one another. The two of you have a connection."

Joshua pulled back infinitesimally.

"Not romantic, but you sense it, do you not?" I didn't want to scare him or put undue pressure on him about the obvious romantic feelings I knew were in his future.

I must've appeared a mad woman with my rush of words. He pursed his lips, seemingly reluctant to answer. "Yes," he whispered. "But I don't know how to describe it."

"You leave for home tomorrow, and there is no proper way for me to share all of this with you. I can promise you that I *am* in control of my mental faculties. I *need* you to hear me."

We both heard the sound of feet on the rock pathway and looked down the trail. Anne was approaching with two glasses of iced tea in hand. I smiled at my granddaughter.

"Hi, it's warm, and you guys have been gone a long time. Thought you might like something to drink." When she reached us, ice clinked as she passed us the glasses, the condensation already running down the sides.

"Thank you," I smiled.

"Yes, thanks," Joshua agreed.

"Is everything okay?" Anne asked.

I looked at Joshua. This was his chance to escape if he didn't believe me. I held my breath during the long pause before he replied.

"Great. It's nice out…nice company, too." He looked at me and winked.

Anne looked at him for a beat or two longer than necessary. She was out here to rescue him I decided. She finally shrugged. "Okay, we are going to fire up the BBQ in a half hour. Maybe you can both work your way back towards the house then? We just prepped some appetizers."

"Sounds delightful," I answered.

Anne turned and headed back towards the house.

I twisted back towards Joshua. "Do you trust me? Are you ready to hear what I have to say?"

He was thoughtful for a moment. "Do you ever feel it…in your soul when something important is happening—even while it is happening?"

I nodded in agreement.

"This is one of those moments, isn't it?"

"I am afraid so, my sweet boy. I am afraid so."

ENTRANCED—A HAIKU

Sleepless nights, your face
Imprinted deep on my lids
Entrancing my soul.

—Robin Woods

JOSHUA: THE STRIGOI

WHAT HAPPENED TO JOSHUA IN ROMANIA?

Thirteen weeks prior to *The Unintended*.

Central Romania

JOSHUA'S POINT OF VIEW

Clutching the Durateus blade in my hand, it suddenly felt foreign. Steel, honed to perfection and inlayed with wood, designed specifically to kill my kind. I'd been told what to expect once they'd lured the Strigoi out of their nest in the cabin not far away. In no uncertain terms—they were monsters. But I wondered, when I faced those monsters, if I'd be able to kill them.

"Move it, leech," the Slayer named Samael spat as he shoved past me to get out of the van. His team member, Kez, radiated the same distaste when he brushed by.

Gabriel grabbed my arm and ushered me outside the vehicle. Without letting go, he marched me a dozen yards away. The cabin was within visual range from here.

"Ignore them," he ordered.

"Yes, Sir," I replied.

He sighed. "I trust you."

I gritted my teeth—he did, but he would kill me without hesitation.

"Speak freely."

"If you trust me, then why do we have two additional Slayers and a team of eight Romanians?" I asked, noting that even the Keeper for the Romanians, Octavian, was here ready to go.

Gabriel scanned over our growing crowd. "It was not my call. Keep focused. *You* are not a monster." He forced me to look at him. "You. Are. Not. A. Monster."

"Yes, Sir," I replied once more. I wasn't sure how he knew what I was thinking.

Gabriel handed me an earpiece. "Put this on. Sebastian is—"

At that moment, the creak of a rusty hinge from the cabin silenced everyone. The sun had set only ten minutes ago, and it was barely tolerable for me to be outside. We hadn't expected any movement until well into the night.

I stuck the comm into my ear. Sebastian was already shouting orders from the command vehicle parked on the crest of the hill above the cabin.

I tried to catch up on the chatter.

"...from nine. One on the move from the east door. Confirm."

Samael: "Confirmed. Moving to intercept."

Gabriel: "Delivering the package to the front."

He was already sprinting towards the truck to grab the body bag full of animal parts and bagged blood to draw the Strigoi out one door. When he'd almost reached it, I used my speed to get ahead of him and take the bait. Flashing to a flat spot about twenty-five feet from the front door. I punctured the first of the blood bags and launched it at the front door, blood spurting as it flew and drenched the threshold.

Sebastian: "Major movement inside."

Within seconds, I had the remaining bags spewing their contents in a line, leading to our carrot. If it'd been human blood, I don't think I could've resisted. I knew my eyes were glowing, and there was nothing I could do to hide them. It confirmed to everyone that I belonged with the creatures of the shadow world.

Sensing the team moving around me into position, I sped back to my spot with Gabriel.

"Next time wait for orders," Gabriel scolded. Then he paused for a moment. "Thank you."

Sounds of shuffling emanated from within the cabin, and the door splintered open. I was horrified—they *were* monsters. Mindless creatures stumbling over one another, tumbling outside. Their shredded clothing was reminiscent of street urchins portrayed in a Dickens novel. They licked at the blood on the weathered floorboards and sucked it from the soil.

I stood frozen, mesmerized by the unreal scene before me, when Sebastian's voice snapped me from my trance. It was then that I noticed Gabriel was no longer next to me and most of the Strigoi had been taken down.

Sebastian: "Three more heat signals inside."

Kez: "I thought it was empty."

Sebastian: "Something inside must be shielding them."

Gabriel: "Entering through the west window."

Octavian: "Alina. Daniel. Protect Gabriel's flank."

Gabriel: "Careful, this structure is not sound."

I forced myself from my stupor, jumping over the headless Strigoi bodies as I ran towards the cabin. I should have been protecting Gabriel, not allowing the Romanians to do it for me.

Storming through the front doors, a sword whirred towards me and stopped a whisper from my throat. Samael growled through his teeth. "Get in the fight or get out." Then grumbled something else under his breath about me being useless .

Samael took two more steps, and the flooring gave out. He dropped waist deep just as another Strigoi burst through the doorway from deeper inside the cabin.

This time, there was no hesitation. I pulled the sword from the sheath on my back and spun in a circle as Gabriel had taught me. The creature had no time to shriek before I took its head. Not allowing my first kill to register, I rushed to Samael and offered my hand to pull him out. He cussed and rejected my help, despite my having saved him.

Refusing to be dissuaded, I reached behind him and broke the board from the floor that was keeping him wedged. He grunted something that almost sounded thankful.

"Gabriel?" I called.

"Back here."

I trotted down the hall, Samael close behind me. It felt as if the cabin was leaning to the left, and I couldn't remember if it had been doing that moments ago.

Gabriel was peering into an opening in the floor. He pulled glow sticks from a pocket in his tactical vest, cracked and tossed them below. A stairwell leading into an underground room became visible. As Gabriel leaned over the opening an eerie glow gilded his face. "Stone walls. They are messing with the heat signatures. Sebastian, did you copy that?"

Sebastian: "Yes. Can you see how large it is?"

Gabriel: "No. Stairs are steep. And Sebastian…it smells like death."

Kez: "I'm on my way."

Sebastian: "Negative. I don't think we should wait until tomorrow to go for the other nest."

Gabriel: "Agreed."

Sebastian: "The Strigoi who tried to escape all moved in the direction of the suspected nest. Kez, you go with second team. Octavian, pick the people you want to send."

Kez: "Affirmative."

The newly formed Team Two switched to a new channel once they'd divided our forces; Sebastian would coordinate if needed. Samael didn't protest at any point, so he must have trusted me enough to remain without Kez as backup. After all was said and done, we had four Romanians on our team: Octavian, Daniel, Alina, and Tatiana, the women every bit as formidable as the men.

Gabriel made a short "tsss" sound through his teeth, getting my attention. He dipped his head towards the staircase, and I followed him. I could feel Samael at my back and hear the near-silent scuffing of the Romanians' feet.

The moment Gabriel's boots touched the dirt floor, a snarl erupted from the darkness—one snarl turned into two and two into three. Mouths full of teeth flashed in the eerie light cast by the sickly yellow glow sticks. Sword circling the air above his head, Gabriel's blade came down with deadly accuracy, taking the head of the first two. I sprang from behind him, rolling on the ground to avoid his blade, and came up in the corner, taking down three more before they could emerge from an opening in the corner.

When I turned back around, Gabriel and Samael were standing over the corpses of a half dozen. It was then I realized that there were two passageways, not one, and they were cave entrances, not additional rooms. The space was larger than I'd expected, about twenty-five feet square, with pillars holding the structure above us made of rough wood. It reminded me of the old mine I'd visited in Gold Rush country in California. Samael had been lucky to have fallen through where he did. If it had been over this room, he would have fallen straight through into who knows what. The tracks in here were fresh; this room had been full of them just minutes before.

Octavian directed the beam of a high-powered flashlight down one the tunnels. Yowls and shrieks emanated from the passageway, and I caught a whiff of singed flesh. Octavian must've been using a flashlight that imitated the rays of the sun—a shudder ran through me. That was something I never cared to experience.

Octavian alternated shining the light down each tunnel, keeping the beasts at bay until a plan was decided upon. Normally, a Keeper would outrank a Slayer, but Gabriel was different. He was from the bloodline of the Angels of the Four Corners. So, when Octavian, Samael, and Gabriel conferred, Gabriel was in charge. I had to retreat to the corner to avoid the light, but my hearing missed nothing.

Dust filtered down from the ceiling, followed by the groan of wood, increasing my desire to go topside. This felt like a tomb —it certainly smelled like one. As Octavian moved the light from one tunnel to the next, I glanced down the darkened one. I caught sight of a glowing set of red eyes. What startled me was the intelligence in them. They didn't belong to a feral animal like the others. I doubted myself for a second. *Vampire eyes are always an exaggerated version of their natural color—not red*. There was a flicker of red before it closed its eyes; I wasn't imagining anything.

I focused and could see the outline of its body with my senses. He raised his arms straight out from his sides and two Strigoi charged under them, straight towards us.

"Octavian!" I yelled.

He immediately shined the light down the other passageway. The creatures didn't shrink back like the others had. They barreled towards us, skin smoking from the light and mouths snapping snarling, both of them heading straight for me. I raised my sword at the ready. Samael struck with efficiency the first one to emerge, severing the head in less than a second. Gabriel defeated the second with the same speed, but there was a third, that'd been masked by the other two, who launched himself over the corpses of the others. The building above groaned once more, dumping coarse dust onto our heads, and that was all it took—that instant of distraction. I swung, missing the head. I spun out of the way as he impacted the wall behind me, then came around, cutting him in two at the waist.

Samael yelled at me, but before I could react, teeth sank into my calf. Gabriel was already there, finishing off the Strigoi I'd chopped in half. The creature had drug its torso over like something out of a zombie movie and bit me. Gabriel roughly grabbed my shirt and pinned me to the wall.

"How do you feel?" he questioned.

"Burns," I gasped, and then concentrated on the sensation. It didn't feel like when I had been turned; this was something else. "I think I'll be okay."

"He could hallucinate and go after all of us," Samael accused.

"It's going away," I said quietly to Gabriel.

He kept me pinned to the wall and stared directly into my eyes. He let go of my shirt and pressed his palm to my forehead, then pulled my chin down to see my teeth. My eyes were glowing, but my fangs had stayed put. I was in control. He exhaled in relief, dropping his hand away. "You are immune to their bite."

"You don't know that," Samael protested.

"How long until a human shows symptoms?" Gabriel asked Octavian.

"Less than a minute."

"Joshua *is* a vampire, so his symptoms should have happened within that time frame—or less."

I dropped my sword and raised my hands. "Permission to check the wound, Sir?"

Gabriel took a step back, giving me space. I noticed Daniel, Alina, and Tatiana take a step back too. All of the Romanians, besides Octavian, had only spoken when spoken to; I wondered if that was normal as I bent down. Pulling up my pant leg, the bite was completely healed, with only the blood left on my skin from the original punctures. The comms crackled, before Sebastian's voice rang out.

Sebastian: "Please report."

Gabriel: "Basement leads to two tunnels. Possibly a cavern system."

Sebastian: "Retreat. Let's see if we can draw more of them out. I want to know what the others find at the second nest."

Gabriel: "Affirma—"

Me: "There's something intelligent down here—it's controlling them."

All eyes whipped towards me, then Octavian started moving the light between the two tunnels a little more quickly.

Sebastian: "Explain."

Me: "I saw something with red eyes. He sent three of them to attack us; they didn't stop, even when they hit the UV light."

Gabriel: "It saw you?"

Me: "Yes. We made eye contact."

Gabriel: "They were going for you, not the rest of us."

I swallowed hard, wondering if the Strigoi master thought I was a traitor for working with the Watchers—if it wanted me dead.

Sebastian: "Retreat as ordered."

Gabriel: "Affirmative."

Gabriel motioned to Samael who, in choreographed fashion, went to the bottom of the stairs to take point for our egress.

Gabriel and Octavian positioned themselves in the rear, closest to the tunnel entrances. Then two things happened at once: a Strigoi came from above, but instead of charging down the stairs, it grabbed onto the beam holding up the left side of the steps, shearing it from the building. The stairs collapsed, the Strigoi falling into the basement with us.

Second, Strigoi came from each passageway headed straight for the columns. Only one of them made it to their target, but it was enough. Beams started buckling under the pressure.

It was almost as if everything was in slow motion; I watched as Gabriel grabbed Tatiana, swinging her into the right-hand tunnel, along with Octavian. Alina dove for the left tunnel, but Samael and Daniel weren't going to make it. Using my speed, I grabbed both of them and flashed into the left tunnel just as the entire cabin caved in.

Growls echoed down the stony corridor, and I realized that this was the tunnel where I'd seen the Strigoi master. *Of course.* Samael cracked a few more glow sticks and tossed them in intervals down the tunnel, holding one up to the wall of debris blocking the entrance. Samael gave me subtle nod in thanks.

I looked at Daniel, he was just a kid. He couldn't have been older than sixteen or seventeen. He was brave though; his dark eyes met mine.

"Any chance you have one of those flashlights that Octavian has?" I asked.

He shook his head. His eastern European accent was much thicker than Octavian's. "No. It's prototype sent by lab to test."

Samael tapped Alina. "You okay?

"Da...yes."

"Keep your eyes on the end of that passage."

"Da." She made a small face for using Romanian, but didn't correct herself this time. Flipping her long braid of dark hair behind her, she moved with efficient grace to her position.

Samael tapped the comm in his ear. "Sebastian? Gabriel?"

A tiny bit of static came through and what sounded like it could have been Gabriel. I walked to the wall of debris and wedged my shoulder against it. With everything I had, I pushed. Wood snapped and there was a low rumble, but I think all I had succeeded in doing was to compact it.

"It's too solid."

Samael shook his head. "We aren't getting out that way."

"Do you think the tunnels connect?" I asked.

"Probably. Let's get moving."

I could taste the fear coming off of everyone. "You want me to take point since I'm immune?" I offered.

"Do it," Samael replied, in an almost civil tone.

I picked up the glow stick on the ground and moved in front of Alina, then paused to tune into my senses. The surrounding sounds of the caverns came into focus and I could hear the heartbeat of all three of them—they were elevated, yet steady. I wished the Strigoi had beating hearts; it would be so much easier to sense them coming. There was also running water in the distance and what sounded like the brush of fabric against rough stone. We started moving.

When I reached the mouth of the cave, my training kicked into gear. Three came at me, but I'd taken them down before any of the others could assist. It opened up into a larger cavern with three more tunnels leading out of it.

Alina spoke. "There is small lake not far. Stream flows from it. This may be source."

"Good. Let's stay to the right and see if we can get to the others," Samael said.

I was feeling anxious about Gabriel and pushed forward without further instructions. I knew Gabriel would kill me if he had to, but at the same time, he was starting to feel like my family. I didn't have any uncles, but that was the closest thing I could think of.

We reached an opening. There was a pool of bubbling water that traveled through the cave for a few yards, and then disappeared underground. It had a lazy current and looked deep.

Alina dropped her extra gear and started stripping down. "I am good swimmer. I check to see if we can get through."

Samael disagreed. "Negative. You could run out of air quickly. I would rather have you in the fight."

Daniel spoke up. "She's like fish. She can do it."

Samael pursed his lips, but agreed. "Watch the entrances."

"I need glow sticks to leave trail," Alina said.

I had six, so I tossed her three. She finished shedding her gear until she was down to a tight, black tank top and what looked like bike shorts, but the texture appeared to be body armor. Then it occurred to me that I was down here with the Romanian equivalent of Lara Croft Tomb Raider, and she was just as hot. I focused on the entry and *anything* else I could think of: pit bulls, bubble gum, movies with lots of explosions, and stale bread. I'd been so focused on losing my humanity that I hadn't thought of a girl in that way in a long time. I'd had chemistry with the medic helping me in the beginning, but she'd been sent away.

"Ready. I'll be back soon." Alina slipped below the surface of the water and glided through the underwater cave in a halo of orange light.

We waited. Five minutes. Ten minutes.

"You think she's okay?" I asked.

"She'll be fine," Daniel answered. He was concerned, though.

Samael narrowed his eyes at Daniel. "You seem young to be on a team like this."

Daniel shrugged. "We start young in Wilds—" He stopped short, as if censoring himself.

I looked back towards the entrance I was guarding and listened intently.

"What, Daniel?" Samael questioned.

"Octavian is my father. This is first mission."

Samael cursed. We had the responsibility of a Keeper's son on our hands—and I liked the kid. Then I realized Alina had the same dark eyes.

"Alina?" I asked.

"My cousin."

I exchanged a look with Samael.

"When we were children, she always bested the male fighters her age. They were not sure if they wanted to beat her or marry her. Our women are strong, but she is jewel in my family. She will come back with way out."

Shadows moved by one of the entrances, but they didn't try to enter. "Do the Strigoi like water?" I asked.

"No, but if cornered, they will go into it," Daniel replied.

"So, we are safer by the water??"

"Theoretically."

Alina breached the surface of the water, sucking in air. She crawled out and stood, bracing her hands on her knees while she caught her breath.

"It not work," she informed us, panting between her words. "Opening small. Maybe Daniel, but maybe no."

Daniel shook his head. "No chance. I'd rather face monster than drown in darkness."

I couldn't blame him. I didn't need to breathe, and I had no desire to go into that dark water. Alina shivered as she pulled her clothes back on, never complaining. Despite the frosty reception when I'd arrived, I respected the Romanians more and more.

We all looked to Samael for direction. He pointed out towards the corridor we had used to get in here. "We will continue in the same direction and see if we can get to the others. Joshua on point. I'll take the rear."

We filed out, and I prayed as I walked, hoping that Gabriel was all right. I didn't want to fail him—or Sebastian. We reached a tunnel that had been blocked by more debris. I climbed to the top of the heap, trying to see into the passageway. Tossing away a few of the stones at the top, air could be felt moving through the new hole. I stared into it and caught the tiniest bit of light.

"Gabriel!" I hollered through the hole.

Samael grabbed my ankle. "Keep it down. Do you see anything?"

"Looks like light from one of the glow sticks." I held up my hand to silence everyone and pressed my ear to the hole not much bigger than a quarter. There was a faint sound of feet, and then, the best sound ever.

"Joshua?" Gabriel replied.

"Yes. Samael, Alina, and Daniel are with me. How about the others?"

"Everyone else is okay. We found a chimney to the surface."

"Can we clear this enough to get to you?"

"Negative. There is a boulder blocking most of the entrance. The rest is too unstable. We will get out and search for another entrance topside. We will not leave you behind."

"Understood." A small amount of panic threatened to rattle its way through my bones, but I suppressed it.

"Be well," Gabriel uttered, warmth in his voice.

"Be well," I returned. It was the first time Gabriel had used the Watcher farewell to me.

I picked my way down to the ground again and relayed the information they couldn't hear. We had no choice. We needed to keep moving and look for another way out. If they had found a chimney to escape, there was bound to be another—there *had* to be.

Daniel dislodged a piece of coal from the wall using two rocks and started marking the tunnels as we moved down them. One tunnel started to blend into the next as we moved forward, always scanning the ceilings for possible openings. We came upon a larger space. There were animal bones and other evidence that this was used regularly.

Alina noticed something and darted off. Before we could chase her down, she had reappeared with two unlit torches. Samael scolded her, but all of us were thankful for her find. We had them lit within a minute. I don't think I'd ever been more thankful to see fire, even with my preternatural vision; this place was murky, at best.

The fact that we hadn't seen any of the Strigoi in a while was starting to concern us. I kept thinking about the red eyes of the one controlling them. My eyes had never turned red before.

I glanced back at Alina and Daniel. "Are vampires with red eyes normal in Romania?"

There was a very long pause before either of them answered. Then, at the same time, they said, "No."

"Zat is what you saw?" Daniel asked, his accent thickening.

"Yes." Their hesitance made me turn again. "What is it?"

"Rumors. Nothing more," Alina clipped.

It was then that I noticed Samael's silence and looked at him. Through downturned lips he uttered, "There is an Ancient down here."

"Wait, what? Like-an-over-two-thousand-years-old type of Ancient?" Terror tunneled its way through my veins. I'd seen video of battles with five-hundred year old vamps. It had taken multiple Slayers to take down one of them.

Samael nodded. "The only documented cases of red-eyed vampires have been from those who were originally cursed— the followers of Moloch. They were cursed around 925 B.C."

I glanced at Alina and Daniel. They both nodded.

"So—a three thousand year old vampire—even better. Anyone have a nuclear bomb in their back pocket?"

Daniel and Alina's eyes met. Then, Daniel rummaged through his bag. He pressed his finger over his lips to silence us and held up several black disks about the size of my hand. After a second, I realized what they were—bombs. They certainly weren't nuclear, but one was strong enough to collapse a single family home and could certainly collapse a tunnel. Daniel had almost a dozen. We could bury that red-eyed creature under enough rubble that it might never get out.

It was the closest I had seen to a grin on Samael's face as he said, "We head back to the main chamber and place the charges to collapse the whole network. We keep one in case we need to," he paused. "We need to…"

It wasn't necessary to finish. Though, an avalanche of rocks would kill humans and Slayers. Depending on how the tunnel collapsed, I could be left to desiccate and suffer for eternity.

I took point again as we followed our markings back to the central nest. Samael took the rear. The added strain of having Octavian's son and niece was heavy. Shadows passed in front of us, so we ducked into a tunnel to the left. We were still headed in the correct direction, so we continued in our almost silent trek. The Strigoi didn't seem to have the same keen sense of smell; otherwise they would have been on us right away.

Time was sluggish as one passage started to blend into another. We were now going up and down and had to crawl some of the time, but I knew we were getting close to the nest. Fifteen minutes later, we made it. We hung on the outskirts, making sure it was still empty. When it was decided that it was, Samael examined the area for a moment and pointed to where he wanted the charges. We set them around the chamber and in some of the nearby junctions. Next, we took the one passage we hadn't explored. If there was a chimney upwards, it wasn't in any of the places we'd been. I just prayed that we weren't headed straight towards the Ancient.

The passage started to narrow, but we continued until we were on our knees, where fresh air was coming through in a steady stream. There were hints of pine and wild herbs. It was the most delicious air I'd ever inhaled. I started moving faster until I realized that I was leaving the others behind. They were getting tired—I was getting tired.

Then, I heard something—actually, it was more felt. There was an ever-so-soft vibration in the rock. A shifting or scuttling. I stopped moving and breathing to listen as the others caught up. There were Strigoi coming up the passage behind us; I could smell them.

I crawled to a larger opening and moved into it. Looking at Samael, I motioned for him to take point. "They are behind us. I'll hold them off."

Samael looked as if he wanted to argue, but he knew I was right. "Just take the rear and keep up. Don't wait for them."

"Affirmative," I nodded.

We started crawling our way down the tunnel, scraping knees, bumping elbows, and tearing ourselves apart to keep ahead of the now audible clamor of creatures behind us.

"There," Samael gasped, out of breath.

A faint amount of starlight was filtering in ahead of us. It looked as if the tunnel opened up into a larger hollow ahead. We tumbled into the cavern, the entrance steep. The floor was smooth and looked like glazed clay. There was a chimney to the surface, but it was a good twenty feet above the cavern floor. I could jump by myself, but the hole was too narrow to jump with someone else on my back.

I met eyes with Alina. "How would you feel about going up there?"

She nodded.

"Samael, give me a knee."

He seemed to know exactly what I was thinking and dropped down beside me. Alina stepped on his knee and then his shoulder. I stood with soft knees and hands on my shoulders, ready to toss her upwards. She carefully climbed onto my shoulders, keeping hold of Samael's hand. He used his free one to hold her other calf.

"You ready?" I asked.

"If you catch me."

"I won't let you fall." And with that promise, I launched her upwards using both my arms and legs. She soared and seemed to hang in the air for a moment, but her fingers just scraped the lower edge of the opening, sending down a shower of dust. I flashed over several yards and caught her.

"Again?" she asked the moment her feet were on the ground. "Can you throw higher?"

I frowned, knowing I couldn't.

"If I had a running start, I could almost make that jump," Samael said. It made sense with his Slayer abilities. I had seen Gabriel jump from the hood of a car onto a roof without straining himself.

Again, Samael and I seemed to be on the same wavelength and not need to discuss logistics. I walked to beneath the opening and hunched down, lacing my fingers into a cradle ready for him. With the sounds of the Strigoi growing still louder, I nodded to him. He ran at me, and at the last minute, stepped into my waiting hands and jumped. I threw him up as hard as I could. He managed to catch one hand on a ledge by the fingertips. He hung there a long moment, and then, like a skilled rock climber, hoisted himself out.

He disappeared for a few seconds, and then lowered his upper body back through the hole reaching down. Daniel appeared at my side and set up to try tossing Alina again. She scampered onto my shoulder. I silently sent up a prayer and with everything I had, launched her one more time. Samael caught her wrist, sure and strong, and pulled her through.

I turned and looked at Daniel. If we could do the same for him, I could make the jump by myself.

Then I felt it again, that odd rumbling, moving sound. We both paused. We needed to do this quickly. I bent a leg and patted it. "I hope you have good balance," I whispered.

Daniel had a thin smile as he placed a foot on my thigh. Just as he started to put his foot on my waiting hand the ground gave way. I grabbed him as we fell, making sure we stayed together, and protected him as much as I could. The floor that had looked like glazed clay was nothing more than hardened mud.

I took the brunt of the impact and let Daniel go when everything stopped moving. We had fallen at least another ten feet. He'd had the air knocked out of him, and he took in breaths in startled gusts.

"You okay?"

"Da," he choked, but then he gasped again. "Arm broken."

I cursed, seeing the obvious break in his forearm.

I looked upwards. Samael was angling himself to jump back in with us.

"No," I held up a hand. "Get rope…and weapons."

The heads from above disappeared, and I could just make out the sounds of hurried footsteps above. I never thought I would miss Samael, but I suddenly felt very alone. Well, if alone means having possibly a hundred Strigoi slowly pressing in on my location.

A torch still burned from above. There was another one still lit on a pile of rubble a few feet away, but the other must have been buried; my sword was gone too. There were three entrances in this chamber in addition to the two above us. The remaining floor from the old room were like sizable balconies. We were very exposed here.

I sifted out everything except the sounds in the cave. The brush of fabric, the crumble of dirt, the scuff of rubber shoes —all of it in no more than a whisper that human ears would never hear. The sounds were coming from all sides. I wasn't sure what they were waiting for.

Daniel made a small sound. He still had his pack, so I dropped to a knee next to him and rummaged through it for supplies to set his arm. I pulled out two stakes, a third fell onto the ground a rolled a few feet away. There weren't any bandages, so I ripped the straps off of his backpack.

I firmly took his elbow in one hand and his wrist in the other to set the bone. "Are you ready?"

He grimaced and nodded.

With a sharp jerk, I reset the bone using my speed and had it lashed to the splint before he could exhale. Daniel made no more than a sharp inhale; he was tougher than I was at his age.

A presence filled the space unlike anything I'd ever felt before, and the hairs on the back of my neck stood up. The Ancient was close. I glanced up at the opening above, praying I would see a rope drop through. I needed to get Daniel out of here—now.

I got up, feeling *it* behind me, and slowly turned.

In the opening to a passageway, a figure stood with glowing red eyes. It was shrouded with a hooded cape. I froze for a moment, and then positioned myself between it and Daniel.

It cocked its head to the side, watching me a moment. I could still see nothing but the red orbs and the outline of the jacket. And when it spoke, I was shocked by the voice. *It* was a woman—or at least something passing for one. Then, she dropped the cloak to the ground. She was tall—pushing six feet, like me. She must have seemed enormous in her time.

"Has Agrona stooped to using Slayers to kill me?"

I was dumbfounded. "Who is Agrona?" I asked before I could sensor myself.

She tilted her head the other way, and I could feel the weight of her stare. I blinked, and she was behind me with my chin cupped in her hand. I hadn't even seen her move. She pulled my head back so she had access to my neck, but at the moment I thought she would kill me, she ran her nose up my neck and nestled it behind my ear. Her free hand was flat on my stomach, pressing me to her. It felt both threatening and sensual.

"No, I smell it now. You have the god himself in your lineage. You must be the pet of a princeling, or perhaps the princess. But I never suspected Agrona would conspire with Slayers."

"I don't know who Agrona is," I managed.

She spun me around and grabbed my face in her hand, almost lifting me from the ground. Her eyes seemed to flash, and the red became more intense. She was trying to control me. "Who sent you?"

I tried to fight answering her, but the intensity of her pull was shutting everything else out. I fought it, but my exhaustion was clawing at me too. "The Council," I answered.

A knife-like grin curled the edge of her lip. "They are using us now? Interesting." She knew it was the truth, and I cursed myself. She loosened her grip and appeared to be thinking. It was then that I realized she was standing between Daniel and me. Despite wanting to look over and see if he was all right, I kept my focus on her. I didn't need to draw attention to him.

The pressure of her gaze increased. "How long have you worked for the Council? Do you know of its inner workings? Do they trust you?"

This time, I gritted my teeth shut and refused to answer. I'd hoped this would deter her, but her smile grew larger.

"Pretties, I have a snack for you," she crooned with syrupy sweetness. Then, she dragged me a step away from Daniel and made sure I could see him.

Growls reverberated down the halls of every tunnel surrounding us—they were low and guttural, but they didn't charge. They were waiting for her permission. I could feel their hunger.

"Please, don't."

"Tell me about the Council," she whispered.

"I'm the first vampire to work with them," I told her; I had to seem valuable to keep us alive. "Let him go, and I will tell you what I know." Of course, that wasn't much, since the Council didn't trust me at all. But if she had survived this long, she was cunning and may make even trivial information deadly.

Before I could react, she'd pulled me in like a ragdoll and had sunk her teeth into my throat. I braced to fight for a second, but she had twisted my arm behind her, locking my body to hers as she drank from me. There was no pain as I'd anticipated; it felt—good. So good it terrified me. I relaxed in her grasp, and despite myself, I wanted more. My breaths became slow and my thoughts muddled. I wondered if opium or heroine felt this good—or was this just the bite of a vampire this old? She was right, I *wanted* to serve her. If she had this much power, why was she hiding underground?

She licked the wound on my neck closed and placed her lips on the shell of my ear. Her voice was seductive. "You will be my pet...and you will do and tell me whatever I want. Your most basic desire will be to please me. I have had kings at my feet, and I will make legions fall before you."

My jaw flexed. I didn't like the sound of being someone's pet, even if she was promising to give me power. She must have sensed this, because she changed her tactic. Despite everything, I was drawn to her. She ran her fingers down my spine. It was as if she was awakening something deep inside me. Her bite had me off balance.

"The blood of your makers must sing to you. You are not a commoner. The Council doesn't even know what they have."

I fought the pleasure stirring in my veins. It was the hormone from her bite. *Fight it, fight it,* I begged myself. There was more temptation in this moment than I'd felt my entire life combined. It would be so easy to give in, and I had no clue about my vampire bloodline. I'd heard Gabriel and Sebastian wondering if my Sire would track me down and claim me, but he hadn't bothered. No. This was not my path.

Closing my eyes, I pictured everything I had to fight with around me. My only advantage was that the Ancient wanted me alive—that I believed. Anything else was probably a lie.

Chances were, that if I attacked her, she wouldn't use lethal force. I'd promised Daniel that I wouldn't let him be turned or taken alive. I would honor that.

I twisted and opened my eyes, gazing at her with awe and obedience. The light in her eyes seemed to brighten. I moved my leg a few inches and stomped on the ground flinging the stake I had dropped into the air. I caught it and drove it into her chest. She stumbled back a few steps, releasing me, and I realized it was from surprise, not because of her wound—I'd missed, and she was out of touch with normal vamps.

At that moment, two things happened. One, the room flooded with Strigoi, and two, gunfire from above sprayed the cavern in arcing circles around me and Daniel. It wasn't killing them, but it slowed and knocked them down.

I dove in Daniel's direction just as rope tumbled from above. Grabbing it, I tied it around Daniel's torso and whirled around to fight off some charging Strigoi. "Pull him up," I screamed while searching for the Ancient, but she had disappeared.

When Daniel had been hoisted to the level of the room above, Strigoi started flinging themselves at him. I jumped the ledge above and fought off as many as I could, but one got past me and severed the rope just above Daniel. He plummeted to the ground and hit hard, crying out on impact.

I jumped down to him, and one of the Strigoi was waiting. It didn't attack, but instead cut a deep gash in his wrist and flung a spray of blood at us. I closed my eyes and turned, but Daniel wasn't that mobile. There was blood on his face, including his lips and eyes. He wiped it away with his sleeve, but when he spat, his saliva looked dark.

"Did it...?"

"Yes," he grimaced. It had gotten into his mouth, now a bite would turn him—and not into something like me. "You kill me if..."

I nodded and looked up. Samael was poised to lower the rope again. I lifted my hand to motion for him to release it when snarls erupted from all around. I let my hand fall to my side and they stopped. Turning in a slow circle, I found her eyes glowing in the safety of a passageway.

"Let him go, and I'll stay," I offered. *It would be easier to escape on my own.*

The rope dropped next to me. I slowly knelt and started tying it around Daniel. She didn't move, and the Strigoi simply growled. I could feel Samael's eyes on me above, and then I caught another scent—Gabriel. He'd made it out and was up there too. I forced my attention back to what I was doing.

I finished securing Daniel and gave the rope a tug, letting them know I was done. I risked a glance at Gabriel. He had a Durateus sword ready to drop in to me, and Samael had the detonator.

My eyes went back to the Ancient. She had lifted her chin as if she was scenting the air; she could probably smell the arrival of another Slayer too.

They started hoisting Daniel back up—slowly, as if they didn't want to spook an animal or disturb the dangerous balance. I could hear the exhales of the people above drawing Daniel back to them. The air seemed to shift, and I made eye contact with the Ancient again. Her eyes flashed brighter for a moment, and her head cocked to the side.

Then, the room burst with activity. That second, a Strigoi moved on me, and Gabriel dropped the sword straight into my hand. Catching it, I spun, cleaving two of the Strigoi in half. A couple of her minions jumped and were hanging onto the rope above Daniel. They kept pulling him up, but with the added weight, there was no speed in it.

The creatures kept coming at me, and I needed to clear enough space to jump to the ledge above. *Maybe I can strip them from the rope.* After taking down five more, I jumped and ran headlong into another horde. I counted each thrust of my blade, trying to keep focused on not dying before I could help Daniel. But it still seemed as if they wanted to capture, not kill me. They weren't brandishing weapons—all the better for me.

Something was swinging, and I glanced away from my opponent. The two Strigoi on the rope with Daniel were now three, and they were swaying in unison, making Daniel swing like the end of a pendulum. The rope was only being pulled up a few inches with each swing. When they had swung to the opposite side, the top Strigoi cut the rope, and they came crashing down.

Daniel groaned and rolled to his side, clawing away from them. I backed up to run and jump the gaping hole to the room above. Just as I started, the Strigoi that had cut the rope dropped to his knees and sank his teeth into Daniel's calf—he would turn.

I jumped and landed, somersaulting to a stop, and without hesitation severed Daniel's leg just below the knee, flicking away the infected limb. I put down the few Strigoi on this side and dove to Daniel. I ripped his belt off and made a tourniquet. He was sweating through his clothes and was barely holding onto consciousness.

He grabbed the front of my shirt. "Kill me."

"No. You won't turn. I'm getting you out." My voice was hoarse and uneven.

Then he passed out. The scent of his blood was overwhelming. I stood, realizing that the Strigoi were swarming again and were climbing about to flood this side. I had to figure another way out. They would just keep cutting the rope and next time, they would probably bite Daniel somewhere I couldn't stop.

Something landed behind me, and I turned, blade extended. Then I stopped short. Gabriel had jumped down with us.

"You should have stayed above," I growled.

He tipped his head to the cave entrance behind him and pointed upwards. He was going to lead me to the chimney they had used. I reached down and picked up Daniel, throwing him over my shoulder, but had to take several breaths to handle the scent of clean blood so close to me. Gabriel was the better fighter; I wanted him free to do just that.

"Need me to take him?" Gabriel offered.

"I got him." My fangs were pressing into my lip, but I refused to give in.

Gabriel didn't argue. He dispatched three Strigoi in our path and led the way. We zigzagged down passageway after passageway, and I knew that I would never have found this on my own. He pushed on with certainty like he'd lived down here his whole life.

We left several false trails at a full run, tossing glow sticks deep into hallways, with Daniel's blood on them. I could smell his blood everywhere, and when I couldn't tell which way to track him, we went to the real exit.

When we reached the chimney, the light outside was changing. "Gabriel," I gasped.

"We still have time."

I nodded and looked up. The chimney was too narrow to keep Daniel over my shoulder, and at least five stories, we were deeper than I thought. Gabriel came prepared, he produced a length of rope and in seconds, tied it around Daniel's torso and looped it between his legs like a climbing harness. Daniel was still unconscious, but moaned as we rolled him back and forth while we trussed him up.

Gabriel handed me the remote trigger for the explosives and climbed up a few feet, motioning for me to hand Daniel over. He kept his body fairly straight and grabbed onto the harness at Daniel's chest. I started climbing up after them, pushing

Daniel up from beneath to take the weight off and speed things up.

Fresh air was filtering in from above, and I could almost taste freedom. I would almost welcome death in sunlight just to get out. Gabriel reached the top.

"Hold him in place."

"Got him," I replied.

Gabriel climbed up the rest of the way, getting onto his hands and knees, and braced himself at the top. He reached in and drug Daniel out into the imminent dawn. I continued upwards, but something caught my ankle. Teeth sank in and I cried out, just as I lost my grip. Gabriel tried for my arm, but I was dragged halfway down the rugged hole, at least two stories worth.

I kicked the Strigoi off and clung to the sides of the chimney, the rough rock rubbing my palms thin. But more of them pressed at me from beneath.

"I am coming down," Gabriel called, dust scattering on me from above.

With another hard yank, I lost another ten feet and felt for the detonator in my pocket. "Don't! Get everyone back. I'm gonna—"

"No. That is an order." I could hear him getting closer.

"Twenty seconds, then I use it, Gabriel. Be well."

"Joshua!" Gabriel screamed. There was a long pause, and then I could hear him climb back out.

I let go, and my sudden weight knocked the half dozen Strigoi under me back down. The second my feet hit the ground, my sword sliced the air with a whir. I had to drive them back enough to either be caught in the explosion or the cave in afterwards. A body fell with each swipe of my sword. The thought of dying terrified me, but dying *for something* didn't seem as bad. I shoved it from my mind.

Then, as if the tide was being drawn out to sea, they retreated. Sunrise was minutes away. Part of me wanted to pursue, but that was probably what the Ancient wanted. I could feel her pull, like invisible tendrils reaching out to me. It was as if the bite on my neck tingled and the last remnants of the hormone she had pumped into me called out for more.

In my head, I counted off the last few seconds, "Four…three… two…one…"

And pulled the trigger.

Click.

The first explosion sounded wet and dull in the distance, but the ground trembled, jarring me out of my stupor. When none of the Strigoi came back in my direction, I flashed to the chimney and climbed towards the growing light. The sound of the cave system imploding grew closer. Small rocks were sheering off above me and pelting me in the face. *The chimney hadn't seemed this high last time.*

About five feet from the top, the tube collapsed. The sides pressed the air out of my lungs, and then the mouth above came down. The last thing I remembered was a large stone striking my forehead and me wishing I was back home in California.

Consciousness came quickly, and I thrashed, feeling trapped. But I wasn't clawing at dirt. A heavy weight stopped me from moving.

"Joshua, stop. We have you. It is daylight. It was the best I could do, buddy," Gabriel said. The weight lifted the second I stopped fighting.

Best he could do? We were in a moving vehicle. I slowly ran my fingers around, and when I got to the zipper, I realized that I was in a body bag. There was a joke in this somewhere, the undead guy in a body bag, but I wanted to know about what had happened. "Is Daniel okay?"

"He is alive. They rushed ahead. They should be at the surgeon by now."

I swallowed. "He's going to hate me," I said, my voice thick.

"No," he paused. "Romanians understand this more than anyone."

"Gabriel, I chopped off his leg. Chopped. It. Off. He's going to hate me."

"He will value his life even more, coming so close to death."

"Is…"

When I didn't formulate a question, Gabriel spoke. "Everyone else made it out fine. It seems most of the cave system collapsed. We lost the van into a sink hole when the main chamber went. No one was hurt. The other team cleaned out the other nest and kept more from escaping into the woods after the cave in."

"Do you think we killed the Ancient that was down there?"

There was a very long pause. "Killed. Maybe. If not, I pray it is under enough rubble to keep it entombed forever."

"Her. It was a woman. She accused me of being an assassin for someone named Agrona."

The vehicle came to a stop, then there were sounds of people getting out and an industrial door closing. Gabriel unzipped the body bag. I got out of it and rolled it into a ball. I sat on the side of the truck bed when I noticed that Gabriel hadn't moved.

"Do you know who Agrona is?"

Gabriel nodded. "She is an Ancient who holds court in France. She is powerful and has many enemies."

"Do you know who we just buried?"

"Did you get a good look at her?"

My neck tingled, and I could feel her against me. Then her image rose to the surface. "Yes. I can give you a full description." I debated on telling him, but I decided I didn't want secrets. "She bit me...I...don't feel any different."

"Were you exposed to her blood?"

"No. I just wish I could have done more...I..."

He seemed relieved. "Her bite will not do anything to you. The fact that you stood up to her at all is commendable."

After some silence, I said, "Thank you."

He sighed, and his hand went to my shoulder. "You did well, kid. I could not have asked for more."

He is proud of me.

My throat constricted with emotion; I hadn't felt like this since my parents were alive. When I had started to wake, there were a few moments that I'd thought I'd been back home and that they were still alive; the knot in my throat tightened.

My mind drifted to what my friend's great-grandmother had told me in Oregon years ago, "Pain is temporary and can forge you like steel if you are strong enough." The Council had trained me to be a weapon against evil. I would be a sword so the world would never have to learn about the monsters that did exist.

ENTANGLED—A HAIKU

In one fleeting glance,
I saw your heart and you mine.
Entangled in fate.

—Robin Woods

EXCERPT FROM THE UNINTENDED
CHAPTER 6—TOO FAR

ALI'S POINT OF VIEW

I felt light-headed; he put one of his hands around my waist and held me up as he turned my body and guided me to the couch, prying my hand from the doorframe.

He flicked the front door shut with his foot and said, "Maybe you should sit down for a moment."

I wanted to go.

I wanted to stay.

Or go.

I was afraid I couldn't control myself, but I literally couldn't stand. I sagged into his arms, and he took on much of my weight, holding me tight.

I didn't want him to stop kissing me, but I did.

His touch made me feel the opposite of what my instincts were telling me. As he backed me across the room, he continued to kiss me as he lowered me onto the couch.

The longer he touched me, the less control I felt. My limbs felt heavier, the odd warmth I always felt from his touch flowing through my body all the way to my toes. He was mesmerizing. His breathing was also ragged.

He kissed my collarbone and then worked his way up my neck and kissed under my chin. Almost involuntarily, I arched my head back as my head grew fuzzier.

I was completely under his power.

He laid me back even more, his weight moving on top of me, his hand unbuttoning the top buttons of my blouse. I couldn't control my breath; I started breathing too quickly.

Hyperventilating.

Too far.

Too far.

No. Too far.

14

JOSHUA: REMAIN IN SHADOW

WHAT HAPPENED IN THE APARTMENT AFTER ALI PASSED OUT?

Twelve weeks prior to *The Unintended*

Outside of London

JOSHUA'S POINT OF VIEW

I puzzled over it for days. My Sire had taken the time to break into my place, but hadn't touched anything. As the sun would be rising soon, I settled into my bed and reached behind my headboard, pulling out the well-used journal—its aged brown leather scratched and softened with use, a tattered, red ribbon marking my place. I snatched my favorite pen from the nightstand and eased back against my pillows behind me.

Closing my eyes I drew in a deep breath and focused my thoughts. I flipped open its pages and prepared to write a response to Ali's latest e-mail, though she would never see my reply.

Feeling a pang for something familiar, I turned to the second-to-last page to pull out the postcard and photo I kept. They weren't there. I skimmed through the journal, fanning its pages and shaking it, trying to loose the items. I whirled through the pages a third time. I felt cold.

I spun onto my knees and shoved the bed from the wall, peering over to see if they'd fallen on the floor behind my bed.

Nothing.

And then it hit me. Time stopped. I ceased to breathe. If my heart still beat, it would have failed. Bowen *had* taken something.

I dashed upstairs to Sebastian to ask him to go to California to check on Ali. He said he would "make a request." I swallowed my pride and begged, but he didn't waiver. He insisted on an appeal to the Council.

That night, every time I closed my eyes I saw Aleria and felt utter panic battering my insides. I'd always felt protective of her, but this was my fault. I may have sent death to her door. I'd already become a monster. If anything happened...

Memories flooded my mind as I tried to lose myself in sleep. I still remembered the day her family had moved into the house across the street, her dark pig tales, and her teddy bear named Stitches who was almost as big as she was. In the evenings, all the kids in our neighborhood would play tag or hide n' seek until the street lights came on, and we had to hurry home. She always managed to hold her own, even though she was the only girl.

Then, all of those thoughts led me down a rabbit trail to something I'd tried to forget—to the summer before I went away to school. Our families had traveled to her great-grandmother's sprawling estate in Oregon. I'd gone on long walks with Aleria's great-grandmother, Mrs. Pryce, each day. She'd told me I would experience great tragedy and that Ali would be part of my life after some of the darkness had settled. She'd informed me that I needed to trust a warrior named Gabriel when he entered my life. She'd even made me repeat his name several times to burn it into my memory. It seemed absurd until—it came true. She'd told me he would give me wise council and protect what I valued most if I could prove my worth.

I still hadn't believed I would see Ali again, even after I'd experienced the accuracy of Mrs. Pryce's predictions. I wished I could go back to that moment in time and record the conversation. I opened my eyes and stared at nothing in particular. I didn't miss the irony that I was now fighting to get back to her. I would do anything to shield her from this life.

The Council deliberated for two days on my petition, and the wait was nothing less than torture. When I asked Gabriel his opinion on my chances, he didn't answer; instead, he gave me a tight-lipped smile and clapped me on the shoulder. He was right—my request was denied. Prejudiced idiots.

I contemplated going without permission, but I didn't want to disrespect Sebastian's or Gabriel's trust. Though I hadn't given up. The squeaky wheel gets the grease—or it gets put out of commission.

Sebastian had faith in my assessment though; he contacted a friend in the estranged Watchers division and burned up some favors. They dispatched a Watcher named Phineas to observe Ali. Sebastian would be contacted if there was any sign of Bowen.

Weeks dragged on with no sign of him, and then, there was.

Bowen was spotted at Campbell Perk, the coffee house that was the backdrop of the photo that'd served as my last link to my old life. He had spent his first two evenings there alone, but the third night he'd spoken with someone—a girl who looked to be 17 or 18, had light skin, was about 5'5", and was "crowned with thick, chestnut-colored hair that fell halfway down her back in waves."

If I had begged to go to California before, those pleas now paled in comparison. I would've set myself on fire if needed. Sebastian relented, against orders, and booked a private plane. I spent every waking moment praying that we were in time, knowing the Watcher dispatched wouldn't lift a finger to save Aleria if Bowen showed any aggression.

While waiting in the private airport, I watched as Gabriel pulled up *The Mercury News* and *San Francisco Chronicle* and perused the local papers on his e-reader. This seemed to be part of his ritual whenever we departed for a new area of the world. I sat next to him with my arms crossed tightly against my chest, glancing at the headlines every once in a while.

I hadn't looked in some time and noticed Gabriel had turned slightly away from me. I leaned forward and read, "Missing Girl Total at Four: Serial Killer?"

I gasped.

Gabriel hit the home button and the article vanished. Without looking at me he spoke softly, "Her name was not on the list."

I swallowed hard. "But they fit her description."

Gabriel didn't answer, confirming my fear, but instead tried to comfort me with, "We will be there soon, my friend."

I rubbed my eyes, hiding the grimace on my face. Not nearly soon enough.

I thought the flight would never land, and in my panicked state, I hadn't considered how they would get me from the plane to the waiting Watcher surveillance vehicle during the middle of the afternoon. Crawling into a body bag while Gabriel carried me was a small price to pay.

Just after sunset, Phineas phoned—he was following Ali and Bowen. Bowen was trying to coax Aleria to enter an apartment. Phineas said Ali seemed hesitant, but he didn't think it would be long before Bowen convinced her to go inside. I could barely dam back the tumult of emotion I was feeling.

We arrived at the location no more than ten minutes later and burst through the door. Two things happened almost simultaneously: One, I took in her crumpled figure on the couch and froze in horror. Her skin looked waxen, so pale it was almost transparent. My world stopped.

And two, my baser instincts overcame me. The smell of blood hit me so hard that I felt my teeth spring instantly; I was blinded to anything but the need to feed.

Pain registered as my head crashed into the door-frame, and I was suddenly pinned against the wall in a steely grip. I didn't fight Gabriel as I struggled to regain control. Shame surged through me as I realized that if Gabriel hadn't stopped me, I would have ended the life of the person I cared about most.

I closed my eyes, afraid to look as Sebastian check her pulse. I couldn't find my voice. After all this I'm too late. I should've come as soon as I found out he was here. *What was I thinking?*

After a few moments, I was finally able to whisper, "Is she—"

"She's alive," Sebastian answered, his voice like gravel.

I pressed against Gabriel's hold.

"No! Stay back!" Sebastian barked.

I still strained against Gabriel.

Sebastian glanced back and added, "Now! I mean it!" I exhaled in a gust and pressed myself against the wall, bearing down until I could feel the sheet-rock groan behind my back.

"She's lost a lot of blood," Sebastian assessed.

I could barely think, let alone speak, out of a fear worse than death. "Did he—"

Sebastian cut me off again, "I don't think so. No, he didn't."

I sighed in relief, and yet still felt sick. If we'd been a few minutes later....

I put my hand on Gabriel's shoulder. "I'm okay; you can let go," I whispered. Gabriel gave me a measured look, then released me.

As Gabriel stalked through the rest of the apartment searching; I still kept myself pressed against the wall and focused on Ali. She looked so fragile...so beautiful. She wasn't the kid from my memory. I clenched my fists until I lost the feeling in my hands as Sebastian finished wrapping her wound. Once he had sealed the punctures with tape, the smell of blood dissipated enough that I could relax a little and allow myself to breathe more deeply.

Gabriel strode back into the room. "He did not leave anything of value behind. A few pieces of clothing, maps of the area, and brochures for San Jose State University." He tossed the papers onto the ottoman and looked at me with an unusual expression, like something was brewing beneath the surface.

Sebastian twisted his mouth to the side and rubbed his bearded chin. "Always one step ahead," he grumbled. He seemed to drift off in thought for a short moment. Abruptly, he looked down at Ali. "It's time to get this young lady home."

"Then what?" I asked.

"Then," Gabriel paused and looked at Sebastian, "we go hunting."

I was pleased to hear those words. *Bowen will pay.*

Gabriel walked over and scooped Aleria off the couch; I took point as we traversed the stairs. The sound of our footsteps reverberated down the cement and wrought-iron staircase. When we reached the vehicle, I opened the door and sat on the bench-seat, motioning for Gabriel to give Ali to me.

"Are you sure?" he questioned. I looked him dead in the eyes. Gabriel returned the look, but gently placed her in my awaiting arms. Sebastian fired up the engine and started driving towards her home as the GPS chirped directions.

Ali murmured a little, and a piece of me wanted her to wake, but then the situation would get complicated. It was better to remain in the shadows. I pulled her against me, breathing in her fragrance; she smelled like home and everything I would never have. I pushed her hair off her forehead, my fingers lingering in her thick hair. I pulled her closer and rested my cheek against hers for a brief moment. I felt more than protective of her. Something much more...

The van came to a quiet stop. Gabriel opened the door and started to reach for her. "I have her. You'll need to pick the lock," I said, pulling Ali just a tiny bit closer to me.

Gabriel nodded, and I followed him to the door cradling her, savoring every last moment. *This may be the last time I see her or touch her.* I felt a pang in my silent heart again.

Gabriel pushed open the door and waited for me to relinquish my hold. "Where is her room?"

"Upstairs on the left," my voice strangled.

I wished I could take her inside, but I hadn't been invited. I placed her in his arms and slowly backed across the front lawn until I was leaning against the massive oak tree in the middle of the yard, watching her window. I wished I could be there when she woke up. Depending on how much she remembered, it could be a very bad morning. Guilt flooded me once again.

Gabriel marched out of the house and urged me towards the vehicle. I shook my head no. He raised his left eyebrow at me. "Do we not have something to kill?"

I nodded. "Yes, we do."

"She will be safe tonight. He knows we have her, and Phineas is on the way to keep watch. He will call if there is any activity."

Reluctantly, I followed him.

I looked back at her house one last time and had the overwhelming feeling that nothing would ever be the same.

15

THE FRENCH COVEN CREST

The original sketch by Robin Woods given to her designer.

The French Coven Crest

The inscription reads: *Mieux Vaut Régner en Enfers*. Which translates to 'Better to Rule in Hell" comes from *Paradise Lost*.

In the epic poem, Lucifer says, "It is better to rule in Hell, than to serve in Heaven."

In *Paradise Lost*, there is a character named Dagan. I used this character in developing my Dagan who is one of the most powerful beings on the planet. He is driven by loyalty, yet is filled with regret.

The fleur-de-lys on the shield directly translates to "lily flower" is a stylized emblem used by the French dating back to the 400s. It symbolizes life and perfection among other things.

The plant on the left is rosemary. It symbolizes remembrance, normally associated with remembrance of the dead at funerals, but also remembrance between lovers.

In my original design, I wanted Rose of Jericho on the right, which is a symbol of resurrection. But, the leaves were a little too ruffly and cluttered the design.

MIEUX VAUT RÉGNER EN ENFERS

SHADOW SELF—A POEM

Darkness swirled inside,
Itching to
Come out and destroy.

—Robin Woods

HUNTED

HOW DID GABRIEL GET HIS SCAR?

Ten years before *The Unintended*

Outskirts of Paris

BRETON AND GABRIEL'S POINTS OF VIEW

Rain dripped from his clothing onto the mildewed hardwood floor; it was the only sound in the condemned four-story apartment. He'd stopped breathing minutes ago, but without breathing, he was giving up his sense of smell. Breton knew that the Slayer was close—too close.

The famed Gabriel had caught up with him within thirty minutes after killing the Watchers and that delicious little Slayer those fledglings had unwittingly served him. He pressed at the still-healing wounds on his chest and neck and shuddered. He'd never been that close to death, and it was blind luck he'd escaped.

Breton had burned every favor owed him to be evacuated to France from England. He wanted familiar ground and aid, but the Queen had denied access to the castle, including assistance from any of her guard, namely his closet friends, Gareth and Cadeyn. She had reminded him that he'd brought the Watchers to her door once before, and this time if he holed himself within 100 miles of the castle, he would forfeit his head. His antics were the reason the guard now killed uninvited guests to the castle.

It didn't matter now. Gabriel had caught up with him again; all his maneuvering had only bought him another ten hours. He was still wounded and half-starved—and in his present condition no match for a Slayer of Gabriel's lineage.

Slowly, Breton took a breath to see if the Slayer had reached the hall in the decaying apartment. *No, but he was still in the building.* His fingers grazed the hilt of his Scottish Dirk. His only weapon, besides teeth and strength, he'd kept the dagger as a trophy after massacring the better part of a clan during one of his binges.

Regret bombarded his mind. If he'd only heeded his friend's advice.

Gareth had said, "Your arrogance will be your undoing. Though Slayers are our mortal enemy, there are consequences in killing them."

"The Queen's leash is firmly in place I see," he'd snarled.

"I agree with her. When Slayers disappear, there can be no trace. Nothing leading to the coven. The Watchers have more power than you give them credit."

"Hence the need to kill them."

"There is always a larger picture, and we still need to live in the shadow world." Gareth shoved at Breton. "Until we are in the open, killing their people indiscriminately will only unite the Watchers and make them more powerful. Keep yourself in check."

A creak from across the hall drew Breton's attention; he pulled his soaking jacket tighter against his body to stop the dripping.

He was tired of running.

He'd never run before. Not like this. There had never been a need.

Gabriel was unlike any Slayer he'd seen in centuries. He was larger and more powerful, and his intellect surpassed his physical prowess. He'd only wanted to make that Keeper pay for ruining his feeding ground; the tiny Slayer had been a delightful surprise.

It had felt so good to kill her and make the Keeper watch. She was strong for her years. He wished he could have savored the taste of her longer. He'd lied when he ate her. He'd told the Keeper that he'd never had Slayer. He'd secretly killed two against the Queen's orders. He hadn't told anyone, not even his friends.

But the most recent female had surpassed all others. If he thought about it, he could still recall her flavor. There was nothing like a Slayer, save a seer, but they had been hunted to extinction. *That was a pity. The ones with the pale eyes had tasted the best.*

The clink of broken glass tore him from his reverie. His fangs had elongated with his thirst. He thought about running again and was disgusted with himself. *No more.*

"Your friends have abandoned you. You will have to face me eventually," Gabriel called out. He was in the hall, no more than two doors down. The smell of the fear billowing from the old vampire reminded him of rancid wine and damp parchment. He wanted the leech to feel him coming, so he dragged his sword down the wall as he approached. Vampires were made of nightmares—but he was what vampires feared, both waking and asleep.

Everything in Breton said, *run, run, run,* but he forced himself to still. Running was against his character until late. He would run no more.

The ting of metal. Step. Drag. Step. Drag. Came down the hall.

Breton shed his fear and reached into the icy depths. He'd survived mobs, fires, imprisonment, and more than one Watcher assault. *What was one lone Slayer?* he asked himself.

Gabriel's silhouette appeared in the doorway, Durateus blade at his side. Gabriel wanted this image to burn into Breton's waking thoughts. *Death was coming for him.*

Breton grinned. "I've killed three of you. You will be my fourth."

Gabriel squeezed the hilt of his weapon, but said nothing.

"Your females are my favorite. Somehow sweeter." When the Slayer didn't so much as twitch, he continued. Hoping that he could goad Gabriel into making a mistake. "I wished I'd had more time with that last little beauty." A guttural sound escaped his lips that should have incited rage.

"Stop being a coward and face me," Gabriel replied. He was ready to finish this, retribution hammering in his head—there was nothing beyond this moment.

Breton bristled at being called a coward and, in a blink, flashed across the room, aiming to knock the sword away from the Slayer. But he sidestepped and used Breton's own momentum to toss him through the wall and into a different dilapidated apartment. Breton was slow to get up, because he knew the Slayer would wait. All the while he chastised himself for making such a novice mistake. Never had he been so rattled by a foe.

He started to laugh as he dusted himself off. "She struggled. She had so much life in her and no fear, so it never spoiled her flavor. Her blood was like sweet wine and meant to be savored. I could've spent days draining her slowly. What was she to you?" He asked, but then something came back to him about her scent and the scent of the Slayer filling the room. They were related. The singular way he'd been tracked. Everything suddenly made sense.

This was vengeance—one of them would die in this place.

He already knew his spree had landed him on a Watcher kill list for sure, but killing a sibling of one of the Four? This was track-until-dead-no-rest-no-quarter.

Panic started to wind its way through the centuries-old vampire. Despite his power, he preferred to ambush from above and not attack head on. The lesser Slayers he'd killed before had never seen him coming because of his ability to mask his presence. And in battle, he'd never fought without others at his side. To a human, he was a god; to this particular Slayer—an equal.

Breton dusted the plaster from his clothing and straightened up. "If I were a betting man, I'd bet she would have lasted a long time. Skin like that, I could have used her for more than feeding." He examined the Slayer, hoping for some chink in his armor. "The first female Slayer I had. I went too quickly. She cried. Can you imagine that? A Slayer, crying. She begged for her life—" he paused for dramatic effect, "and for me to stop touching her."

The Slayer swallowed, and Breton's eyes tightened a split-second before he charged his enemy. They grappled, turning and smashing into walls, back and forth, again and again. When they finally broke free from one another, they were both injured and panting. Then, Breton realized that the Slayer had more than stabbed him; his wound wasn't healing as it should have been, and blood loss was weakening him further.

A morbid laugh echoed in the abandoned apartment. The Slayer was using the drug his own vampire queen used against criminals. Before he could wonder longer as to how a

Slayer had procured such a thing, he narrowly missed the Slayer's next blow. Desperation started to fuel Breton's thoughts. *Goading him wasn't working.* "Members of my coven will be here presently."

"You are alone. Your coven cut you loose long ago," Gabriel said, as he made sweeping slashing motions with his sword, driving Breton into a corner. He was getting sloppy in his stance but didn't care as long as the vampire perished.

Breton glanced side-to-side; there was nowhere to run except through the Slayer. It was no longer rainwater dripping on the floor but his own blood. He took two rushed steps towards the Slayer, then pivoted and shouldered his way through the window. Glass exploded from it in a deadly shower as Breton launched himself through the fourth-story window. He seemed to hang there for a moment, and then plunged downward, landing on his side in a sick thud. Rolling onto his hands and knees, he crawled towards the opening of the wide alley, hoping to recover enough to run before the Slayer had time to take the stairs. But the Slayer didn't take the stairs. Something landed two meters from him with the lightness of a jungle cat.

Dragging the dirk from its sheath, Breton succeeded in jerking to the side and knocking away the Slayer's sword. But he already had a short blade in hand. Breton managed to kick the side of the Slayer's knee, and he came crashing down, obviously more injured than he had appeared.

It was a desperate type of fighting, resorting to jabs and scratches as they rolled, grappling once again—both huffing from exhaustion, emotion, and injury. Finally, the Slayer managed to wedge his Durateus blade in Breton's sternum, one angled push and Breton would be paralyzed. But at that same moment, Breton angled his dirk for his foe's eye and missed, embedding the tip under the Slayer's cheekbone.

They were at an impasse. If Gabriel pressed the blade into Breton's heart, Breton would be able to reach Gabriel's eye. So they stayed locked, each shaking with an effort to finish and maim the other.

"If you have any other family, they are not long for this world," Breton choked.

Gabriel didn't respond, but rather gave the blade one last shove into Breton's heart, knowing the cost. Breton's dirk carved a long, fishhook swath in Gabriel's face before paralysis struck the aged vampire, then the dirk clattered to the damp ground.

Without ceremony, Gabriel stood, limping to his sword, and took Breton's head. He heaved the body into a dumpster, leaving it there until he could contact Cleaners for removal.

But the anger still burned his insides. He thought he'd feel better afterwards—but none of it brought his sister back.

GABRIEL: LIVE WITH THAT

WHAT ENDED GABRIEL'S RELATIONSHIP WITH CHLOE, THE BEAUTIFUL, TATTOOED GIRL?

GABRIEL'S POINT OF VIEW

Chloe closed her eyes, tears plummeting unchecked from her cheeks, her makeup now tiger stripes down her face, and I was the cause. Silence stretched into the night when I did not know what I could offer.

She broke the quiet, hugging a couch pillow to her chest. "After they found my brother and your sister, I'd kissed you and asked you to kill anyone involved. I'd already been half in love with you. Then, I got the call from Miller." She swallowed. "They'd found you after you'd called for the Cleaner. He said you'd tried to bind your face, but you were in bad shape—a bruised kidney, knife wound to the side, various punctures, bone-deep bruises all over your body, and he wasn't sure what else. If you were anything but a Slayer, you'd be dead." She fell silent again.

I knew she was reviewing the past for a reason, so I waited.

"When you were airlifted back and I saw you bandaged and delirious, I knew I wasn't half in love with you. I was all in. I wanted you completely. You'd been my friend and confidant for so long, but it took our shared loss for me to finally kiss you. But now..." Her voice trailed.

Again, I waited.

Seconds stretched into minutes, and when she had left her statement unfinished for over ten minutes, I prompted, "But now things are different."

"I don't want them to be." Fresh tears played at the edges of her lashes.

I kept my eyes off of my bandaged thigh, knowing my new injury was the catalyst for old hurts.

She dropped the pillow and slowly moved across the room, standing in front of my armchair for a long moment. With care, she straddled me, being careful of my leg, and stayed on her knees so that we were nose-to-nose. Her small frame appearing so fragile tonight.

Chloe's lips parted and my eyes went to her mouth, waiting for the words, but she did not speak. Leaning in, she brushed her lips against mine, shallow breaths punctuating each gentle kiss. Her tongue entreating me to kiss her more deeply. Grabbing fistfuls of my hair, she controlled the kiss—slow, intense—waking my desire for more. I wanted to trace every tattoo on her body with my tongue and to make everything better. I wanted to make her forget all of her troubles. I wanted us to feel whole again.

"I love the way you taste," she murmured against my neck.

"Chloe," I breathed, kneading her hips with my hands.

She pulled off my shirt and began to trace the scars with her fingertips, still careful not to sit back on my thigh. "For two years we've done this dance. I know you love me, but…" Her voice quivered, and she stopped speaking.

I captured her mouth with mine, initiating more contact. My hands rising to her ribcage, then my mouth moving to her collarbone. She was my refuge, my touchstone to keep the warrior in check. "I love you." I did not say it often enough, preferring to show her.

"I've always felt your love, even before we were together. But I need this to stop. There's this darkness…no recklessness, inside you now. Ever since Laylah. Gabriel, I don't want to lose you." She unbuttoned her shirt, letting the silky fabric slink to the floor.

It became hard to focus on anything but her perfect, honey skin. I hugged her to me so that I could feel her flesh against mine. I wanted Chloe so much. My body strained for this fierce woman. My very soul wanted to be close to hers.

She rested her mouth next to my ear and whispered, "I'm leaving the Watchers, and I want you to come with me."

I stopped kissing her and froze.

Silence stretched out once more, and she eased back to see my face.

"Leave?"

"I'll be an Asset and help out when needed, but I'm done with the missions. I'm done sitting in Command watching you risk yourself. There is this part of you that wants to die, and if you did, a huge part of me would die with you. I need to leave the Watchers to save myself. I want to save *you*."

"No Slayer has ever left."

"It doesn't mean they can't," she said.

"My life, my purpose, everything is part of the Watchers. My lineage created what we have. It is *me*. How do I leave that?"

"For me."

We sat in silence for a long while, staring at one another.

"I—" She put her fingers over my lips to stop my words.

"Take me to bed. Make love to me," she whispered.

She eased off my lap, holding my hand, as she led the way.

I followed her to our room, knowing that when I woke, she would be gone. Knowing that the Slayer would become my whole and I would have to live with that.

19

ALI'S LETTER TO JOSHUA

WORRIED THAT HER VISION OF TYRAN KILLING HER WOULD COME TRUE. ALI WROTE JOSHUA A LETTER AFTER THEIR SECRET WEEKEND AWAY.

From *The Nexus* Chapter 22

Joshua—my dearest love, my Ferdinand,

I have fallen in love and it is forever.

> *How do I love thee? Let me count the ways.*
> *I love thee to the depth and breadth and height*
> *My soul can reach, when feeling out of sight*
> *For the ends of Being and ideal Grace.*
> *I love thee to the level of everyday's*
> *Most quiet need, by sun and candle-light.*
> *I love thee freely, as men strive for Right;*
> *I love thee purely, as they turn from Praise.*
> *I love thee with a passion put to use*

In my old griefs, and with my childhood's faith.

I love thee with a love I seemed to lose

With my lost saints, --- I love thee with the breath,

Smiles, tears, of all my life! --- and, if God choose,

I shall but love thee better after death.

—Elizabeth Barrett Browning

The air seems to be electric, charged with energy of an upcoming storm. My present happiness makes me dread what I feel is coming. I know you feel it too despite your protests.

I know I have said it a million times before, but I love you. More than my own life. You are a part of me. Something I need more than air, food, or water. You have said that I am your North Star, but to me, you are my sun. When I think of you I am bathed in warmth. You are what has kept me going.

The last two days have been—perfection—the best in my life. I wish that we could stay here forever and stave off all the monsters that want to steal our very souls. And no arguments...you have a soul. Your goodness is proof of that every day.

If something happens to me I don't want you to lock yourself in sorrow. Live for both of us. The world needs you.

I have no regrets. Only want of more time with you.

Yours in this life and the next,

Miranda

20

EXCERPT FROM THE NEXUS CHAPTER 27—BIT BY BIT

SPOILER ALERT: READ BOOKS 1-2 FIRST

The French Coven Dungeon

ALI'S POINT OF VIEW

I was curled in a fetal position in the corner for a long while. Counting the stones on the opposite wall of my cell, trying to ignore my hunger, my pain, my helplessness, when I was jarred from my daze.

There was a commotion down the corridor, and a voice said, "Sire, please. No one is allowed down here."

"She's here, isn't she?"

"Prince, please, we were given strict orders!"

And then, a body flew by the door and crashed into the dead end, followed by another, and then another. The door was wrenched from its hinges.

I didn't think I would be happy seeing him, but I was. Bowen entered, his presence the opposite of his brother's. He lifted me into his arms and carried me from my place of darkness. I latched onto his shirt like it was my lifeline. I closed my eyes and allowed myself to feel safe.

21

BOWEN: THE PRICE

WHAT PUNISHMENT DID BOWEN TAKE FOR ALI?

SPOILER ALERT: READ AFTER THE NEXUS

During **Chapters 27 & 28 of** *The Nexus*

In the French Coven

BOWEN'S POINT OF VIEW

A gentle knock at the door wrenched me from sleep. I hadn't slept for almost thirty-six hours, my wits were dull, yet I knew what this was about. I'd been waiting.

I'd stolen Aleria from the dungeons, and I was surprised it had taken eight hours for them to come for her. Debating, I stood, pressing my thumb and index finger to my forehead. If I waited too long to open the door, they may burst in, putting me on the defensive. My mother would arrive with enough of the guard to overpower me if I wasn't careful. Or more likely, with people I would not be willing to cause any permanent damage.

"Belenus," I heard in not much over a whisper. It wasn't who I had suspected.

I cracked the door open. Morpheus was leaning against the wall just outside the door. He was expressionless. When he didn't explain his reason for being outside my room, I questioned, "What is it you want?"

"I came to warn you, Cousin. Your mother heard about your heroic gesture and has ordered Gareth to gather some of his men." He pointed to the windows in my corner room. "They will enter through the windows on both sides and through the door. I would get ahead of this. Your little pet may be put back on a leash."

I grabbed his shirt front and dragged him inside. Once the door was shut, Morpheus shoved at me and tugged at the bottom of his shirt, straightening it. He looked around the room with a question on his face.

I pointed to the bed with the drawn curtains. "She is sleeping."

His shoulders relaxed. He may have been worried I had smuggled her out somehow. I turned away from him and rubbed my temples, thinking. "I promised her that she would be safe in here."

"*Safe*—you do know your mother's plans, do you not?" he asked in a harsh whisper.

I turned back and pinned him with my stare.

"You really like this little human," Morpheus commented as he strolled towards the bed.

"Morpheus," I warned.

He raised his hands. "I promise not to touch, Belenus. Tsk, tsk." He drew the bed curtain back and stared at her sleeping form. "She doesn't look like much now, does she?"

"Meaning what?"

"Humans are fragile. I wouldn't get attached. She faintly resembles what was brought in here weeks ago."

"So you *have* seen her."

"Briefly, when she and Taranis arrived. Icelos and Phantasos thought her brave little front when she saw us quite humorous. She was much prettier then."

"You should have told me that they brought her in."

Morpheus sighed, his trademark scowl darkening his features. "I am warning you *now*. You know I don't like to get in between your squabbles. But, I find the girl…" He focused on her again.

"Find her?"

He tilted his head in my direction. "Familiar."

His response surprised me. "How?"

"I am not sure. I have to admit, she is a fighter. Even in the state to which Taranis has reduced her, she fights us in her dreams. I have never seen the like."

If I wasn't mistaken, his expression was one of respect. *But Morpheus doesn't respect humans.*

"I am concerned, Cousin. This isn't like your other disagreements with your brother, is it?"

"I'm afraid not."

"Please tell me you do not love her!" he hissed.

"No. No...I am fond of her, but as I told...someone else, I feel *compelled* to protect her. There is no other word."

"Who might you have said that to?" He narrowed his eyes.

"It doesn't matter," I replied dismissively. *If my mother knew that I had warned a Slayer, I would already have been dead.*

"Put her back, Belenus. Make peace with your brother. Appease your mother. She has missed you. She needs to see some show of compliance before she will trust you again."

"She doesn't trust me?"

"You ran off for three-hundred years. You are in some feud with your brother. You disappear for days without a word, so your mother is in fear that you are going to disappear again. She blames the girl for your recent behavior."

"And how have you come upon all of this recent information?"

Morpheus backed away from the bed and descended the steps, shrugging. "Do you *want* to know?"

"If it has anything to do with the reason you were taken out of the succession for the throne, then no."

The edge of his lip turned up.

"I really don't want to know." I looked towards the bed. Aleria looked so small, huddled in my sheets. "How do I get ahead of this?"

"Go to your mother, now, before your brother returns."

"So her men can steal Aleria away while I have an audience with her? *No.*" Anger stirred inside me. "Are you manipulating me to get me to leave?"

There was a flash in Morpheus' eyes. My question struck bone. "Have I ever misled you?"

"I am sorry, friend. I should not have asked."

"No, you should not have. I know that I went to ground not long after you left for the New World, but my loyalties have not changed. You are a brother to me."

"Again, I apologize." I sighed. "You have the ear of my mother. How should I approach her?"

"You won't like it."

I blinked at him.

"Your human is worth this? She will be dead by Spring."

My throat constricted. "I won't leave her to my brother's devices in that dungeon for months. I won't. She deserves better than all of this." I walked back to the bed to check on her once more before making my decision. I couldn't hear her breathing or her heart beating. Panicked, I checked the pulse on her neck. Her heart rate was slow, but it was beating.

At that moment, Morpheus was on the other side of the bed, examining me. "Are you sure you are not in love with her?"

"Twelve evenings. That is how many times I was able to see her in thirteen days before my brother injected himself. Our kind does not come to love a human that quickly."

"And what did you *do* for those twelve evenings?"

"We talked."

"I thought I was the only one you talked to." His scowl turned swoony. It didn't look right on his face. He was making light, but there was truth to his statement.

I talked to few people, Morpheus probably more than anyone else. Yet, Aleria had somehow...maybe it *was* her Lux blood. I summoned images of her, sitting in that café, surrounded by piles of books with a determined expression on her face. Then of the hours I sat quizzing her for her tests until the coffee shop would force us out at closing. I had dreaded those moments. I would walk her to her car so slowly that she would chastise me for it. I couldn't help myself.

Morpheus drew me out of my reverie. "Bowen," Morpheus murmured. It was the first time he had used my new name.

"We talked, but that is all. She is funny and passionate and surprising and so, so very…good. I need her forgiveness. By allowing Taranis into her life, I have stolen everything from her."

"You did not touch her after you took her from the dungeon?"

"Is that why you are here? To find out if she is *pure* for the sacrifice?" It was my time to feel wounded. "She hates me. Of course nothing happened last night. And how is it that everything is resting on me?"

Morpheus casually put some space between us. "She was checked nine days before your brother brought her in. She was a virgin."

"You *checked?*" I was incredulous and felt violated for her.

He held up his hands in surrender. "It was part of your mother's plan. After your human was poisoned, they implanted a tracking device, harvested what was needed for me and mine, as well as, for her pet project, and made sure her chastity was still intact."

Aleria stirred, and we both turned to watch her, but it was obvious that she wouldn't wake anytime soon.

Morpheus continued, "In order for your father to harness the powers from a pure sacrifice, there are extra preparations to make."

"What pet project?" I asked.

When Morpheus told me what else they had done to her, I had to sit. There was no limit to my mother's scheming.

I looked up at Morpheus, my anger simmering. "What is your idea? How can I convince my mother to keep her with me?"

"*Succedaneum.*"

I froze.

"I doubt your mother with take anything less."

"You are right, of course." Before Morpheus had a chance to draw a breath to speak again, I had his shirt in my fist and had slammed him against the wall. "I will go, but you will stay outside and keep watch. No one. Not my brother. Not my mother. Not ANYONE will enter. And you will damn well stay out of her head. If you or your brothers tamper with one more dream, you will grieve the day."

"What if she wakes and asks your whereabouts?"

"She won't. And she will never know about this. As far as she is concerned, I never left the room."

"You will *lie* to your human?"

"Yes. She will not bare this burden, as well." I let go of his shirt, but he didn't straighten it this time. I glanced back at Aleria one last time before leaving the room. There was an awful, hollow feeling in my chest.

Once outside, I shut the door, and Morpheus leaned against the wall looking at his nails. I started down the hallway, but Morpheus called after me.

"Belenus, you will fall in love with her, if you have not already. It will only make it more unbearable when your mother sacrifices her. You do not move on well, Cousin."

My pace quickened, trying not to let his words settle in my mind. When I reached the throne room, the doors were open. Gareth, the Captain of the Royal Guard, was nowhere to be seen, and Mother's beady-eyed assistant was missing. Cadeyn, Gareth's younger brother and second in command, was in the doorway, but he didn't look surprised to see me.

When I was a few meters away, I asked, "Where is your brother, Gareth?"

Cadeyn narrowed his yellow eyes. "Off serving our Queen."

"I need an audience with my mother."

"She was hoping you would stop in." Cadeyn held a pleasant look on his face, but I knew him well enough to know that he wasn't comfortable.

I entered, and the door was quickly shut behind me. My mother sat at her desk at the base of the steps to the throne. She was dressed all in black, as if in mourning. Nothing flashy. No jewelry. *This was not right.* I glanced around the room. There were no advisors or familiars. For the first time since I had returned, we were truly alone.

She didn't look up from her papers. I walked to the middle of the vast room and knelt on one knee. "My Queen." When she started to look up, I quickly bowed my head.

Mother didn't say anything, but I heard the slow click of her high-heels drawing closer. She could approach silently if she chose, yet she didn't. I wasn't some sycophant that could be intimidated, though.

I was, however, surprised when she crouched in front of me and grabbed my face. "Someone has informed me that you have been a bad boy," she patronized as if I was a child.

"I did not mean to offend, my Queen."

"You really must want something, my love." Her grin was so sharp, it could cut glass. I never called her "Queen" unless in the presence of visiting dignitaries. I swallowed as her fingernails cut into the skin of my cheeks.

"I ask for permission the keep the Seer in my custody until the time of the sacrifice."

"Don't you mean, *in your bed?*" She let go of my face and stood.

"On a literal level, she is, but I give you my word that I will not join her."

"Why should I believe you when you have defied my orders?" she scoffed, baiting me.

I grit my teeth. "I did not give you my word before. I am sorry if I have offended."

She started walking in a slow circle behind me. "On both of your knees, please."

I eased onto my other knee. My back tingled with her behind me. I listened, but could not locate her—she had stopped breathing, and her heels were no longer clicking against the marble.

"Why would I allow it?" She spoke from directly behind me.

"*Succedaneum.*"

She went silent again. I counted the seconds, waiting for her answer... one... two... three... four... five... six... seven... eight... nine...te— The whir of splitting air stopped me short. I held my breath, just as the whip lashed at the flesh on my back.

It was so much more painful than I had remembered. I spotted a droplet of blue, iridescent liquid that had been knocked from the whip. She had dipped it in Pyralis to prevent me from healing too quickly. She was angrier than I had realized.

I heard the whir again and braced myself. She struck me three more times, the metal tip biting harder with each successive strike. It was four in total before she bothered speaking to me.

"One for defying me, one for taking what is rightfully your brother's, one for breaking my dungeon, and one to pay for her first night's rent. You asked for *Succedaneum.* You can be her substitute for as long as you pay. I will see you tomorrow. This will increase by one for each day. If you cry out, I will assume it is for mercy, and she will be sent back. Am I *clear?*"

"Yes, Mother," I finally gasped. I was trembling and found it hard not to fall forward...or hold my tongue.

"What is it, Son?"

"I just wished you had warned me. I liked this shirt." When the whip struck me this time, I did fall forward, but I didn't cry out. I wasn't sure why I had let my words slip.

"Get out of my sight," she spat.

"Yes, Mother. Thank you for your mercy," I choked out. The words felt like acid, but I had gotten what I had wanted. Aleria was mine. For now.

I labored to my feet and walked to the door. It took all of my strength to walk as if I wasn't in pain. The second I was outside, Cadeyn shut the door, blocking my mother's view. I grabbed his arm to steady myself.

"Let me see," Cadeyn ordered, his face stoic.

"Call off Gareth. She's mine."

Cadeyn allowed me to hang onto him for support as he placed his phone to his ear. "Belenus is with me. It has been called off...No, *Succedaneum*." He hung up and promptly leaned around me. I felt his fingers on the shreds of my shirt. In a hushed tone, he asked, "She used Pyralis on you?"

"I was always curious as to why they chose a name meaning 'of fire'" I quipped, but my pained voice kept it far from being humorous.

"Let me call someone to help you back to your room; I can't leave my post." Cadeyn face was no longer stoic.

"No. No one knows except you and Gareth. I will see you tomorrow."

"Tomorrow?"

I didn't respond, but it was readily apparent when he understood my meaning: This was not going to happen just once.

I started in the direction of my room, but Cadeyn stopped me. "Wait." He trotted over and took off his guard's coat. "Put this on so you don't leave a blood trail."

I glanced at the floor. Random splats of my blood littered the stone. I raised my arms, and he helped me into the coat. I managed to stumble all the way to my room without running into anyone. I prayed tomorrow and the next day I would be so lucky.

When I opened my door, Morpheus grinned, "Did she take your title and make you a guard in..." He didn't finish.

I fell to my knees again. "I need the antidote to Pyralis to prevent scarring. Can you get it for me?"

"Damn your mother." A few more curses slid through his lips as he stood up. "I will be back with everything you will need in a few minutes."

I bent forward until I was on my stomach on the floor. The cool marble easing some the fire. I forced myself to stay awake, afraid that Gareth would creep inside and step over my body.

True to his word, Morpheus returned with a water basin filled with supplies. He ushered me into the bathroom, never letting go of my upper arm, and had me sit on the ledge of the tub.

My shirt was stuck to my back, so I needed help shrugging

out of it. Morpheus' voice was uncharacteristically thick: "I will have to stitch a few places before using the antidote if you don't want scarring."

"Do it."

He rearranged my flesh as I sat still. When he had finished the needed repairs, he poured several liquids into the basin and dipped a sponge into it. The moment he dabbed the mixture onto my back, the fire eased. I let out a gasp of relief. *I could get through this.*

"So this is it? She stays with you?"

"Morpheus," I paused. "I will need your help each day after Aleria goes to sleep."

Morpheus took a few labored breaths. "She is worth this, Cousin?"

I stared at him. "She cannot know."

"As you wish. I have a familiar that I glamoured outside. You will feed, and then you will sleep for a few hours. I will stay. If she starts to wake, I will rouse you and be out of the room before she is fully conscious."

"No, Morpheus. I ca—"

"If you need my help, this is what you will do. She never need know that I was here."

I showered once my wounds had closed. When I entered my room once more, Morpheus had the familiar on the waiting for me. As I fed, he cleaned the signs from the bathroom. He emerged just as I had finished feeding and sent her away. She wouldn't remember a thing. I couldn't have asked more of him.

"Sleep," he ordered.

I nodded, walking to the couch and stretched out on my stomach. Sleep came quickly.

Someone shook me. "I apologize, Cousin. I must go."

I rubbed my eyes and glanced at my watch. It had been four hours. "Thank you. Has she stirred?"

"No."

"I will see you tomorrow then."

Morpheus hesitated. "How many days of this can you take?"

"As many as needed," I replied.

Morpheus stared at me with disapproval for a long moment. "I will see you tomorrow."

When he was gone, I settled in for my vigil. I wouldn't be able to rest much until things were settled with my brother, despite reaching an agreement with my mother. I didn't allow myself to sleep and had to continually check to see if she was still breathing to ease my fears. After another eleven hours, my lids became heavy. I remembered closing my eyes, but not drifting to sleep.

I woke, and my eyes drifted to the bed. Panic seized me. I stood and spun in a circle—she wasn't here. "Aleria! Aleria!"

"I'm here," a small voice called from the bathroom.

I was at the door. "Are you all right?"

She opened it. "Yes, thank you. Sorry."

I was still trying to calm my panic. "No…I just thought…"

She grinned at me. "That I had been snatched away."

"Yes, I shouldn't have slept," I replied, angry with myself.

"You can't stay awake 24/7," she scolded me. "How long did I sleep?"

"Over a day. I worried that you might not wake at all." Worry spilled into my voice.

"Then it was good you slept." She smiled again and lightly touched my arm. The smile was genuine. I looked down, trying to hide my shaky exhale.

When I had pulled her out of that cell, she had told me that she had spent five months hating me. But it was already apparent that those feelings were waning.

My last moment with her in California, I had told her that she would always be part of my heart. Morpheus was correct. I released another shaky breath. I was going to fall in love with this girl, and it was going to cost me more than I could imagine.

BOWEN: ONE LOVED

WERE BOWEN AND TYRAN EVER CLOSE?

France, the Middle Ages

BOWEN'S POINT OF VIEW

Taranis grinned at me conspiratorially moments before our mother strode into the room. It was evident that she was in one of her moods and not to be trifled with. The day had been nice while it had lasted. I suppressed an eye roll.

"Belenus, you need to control your people."

Taranis placed his hand over his heart in faux concern. "Yes, Brother. You should get on that. What are they up to now, Mother?"

She overlooked his insincerity and kept her gaze on me. If I hadn't already ruled my land for a century, it would have made me squirm. I was beginning to regret my visit home. It was my first time returning since losing Amée almost a year ago—the grief and guilt still as tangible as the sky and this very castle.

"They aided known Watchers. Use the plague as a cover. Kill them."

I tried to keep the temper out of my voice. "And whom shall I kill?"

"My informants tell me the inn keepers, blacksmith, and the physician."

Swallowing, I asked with caution, "Did they know they were assisting Watchers? Any stranger could have come to town for a service, stayed in the inn, and seen a doctor."

"You question me?" Her eyes the blade on which I stood.

Taranis chuckled. "I think he questions the sycophants trying to garner your favor with bits of tasty information."

"Crippling one of my villages is also a concern," I answered.

"Do we know where the Watchers are located?" Taranis asked, still aiding me as a buffer.

She raised a brow. "They are of secondary concern. Killing those who aid them will drive them from our lands."

Secondary concern? Does she know who she is asking me to kill? "I will pack my things immediately." I bowed and exited.

When I rounded the corner, I paused, listening to my brother. He cooed to my mother, "Do you really need to send him away only a week after arriving? It has been good to have him home."

I walked on to ready myself for my journey, not waiting to hear her reply. *It had been good to see my brother. The competition my mother had been so careful to promote had waned in my absence. Why she wanted us at each other's throats was beyond me. As a team, we were almost unstoppable.*

When I was almost packed, yet still reeling at the "who" I had to kill, Taranis strolled in looking like he'd won some sort of competition. Before the door closed, I noticed a trunk outside.

"A parting present?" I asked, managing a grin.

"The best present of all. I'm coming with you."

"Yes, much more valuable than gold. Wait, sorry. I was confused. I would much prefer gold. Or dirty linens."

Taranis grinned. It was the grin that always got us into trouble when we were younger and I usually bore the brunt of the payment. "Up for a game of Hide and Seek?"

I furrowed my brow in question.

"I know why you hesitated about the killing," he admitted.

"That province relies on those men. And you know that mother means me to kill the entire family. It—"

Taranis placed his hand on my shoulder to silence me. "We will away together and find a solution." He allowed seriousness to rest on his brow for only a moment, and then bowed dramatically. "I shall summon the coach."

I blinked, and he was gone. Exhaling, I wondered what I would regret most.

Clouds thick with rain blocked most of the moonlight and bathed the cluster of buildings in ominous light. The carriage crept along the rocky main street leading to my castle, humble in comparison to my mother's monstrosity. My instincts warned me about something, and when I glanced at my brother, I knew I was not wrong.

"Do you smell it?" Taranis whispered.

I stopped and took in a slow breath. *Vampire. Correction: Two. And the musk of several human strangers.* "For us? Mother's spies? Coincidence?"

Taranis' mouth flattened into a hard line. "We can't be caught inside the carriage."

I knocked on the ceiling, "*Serpentipedi.*" (Latin: Serpentine)

Immediately my coachman sprang into action. We picked up speed and whipped around a bend; the second we hit a blind corner, Taranis and I jumped from the carriage, hiding behind some empty barrels. My coachman continued using an evasive pattern as if we were still inside and headed off towards the castle.

We crouched, each on a bended knee, for several minutes. Waiting. The air shifted slightly, bringing with it new scents. I recognized those of some of the villagers—and fear. I was perplexed and looked to my brother. The smell of the blacksmith's forge permeated the air, and it was out of character for him to be working this long after dark.

Taranis had his head cocked to the side, listening. "This may be coincidence."

After hearing the accents of the strangers, I agreed. "The Duke of Burgundy's men. It doesn't sound like the *Raubritter* (German: Robber Barons) we chased off months ago." I thought for a moment, then added, "They want to expand their territory again. I wonder if Watchers were here at all?"

"Mother wants your people dead," Taranis reminded me.

"Not if I can hand her the Duke's men."

Taranis nodded, but his expression didn't align with the assent of his nod.

"I'll send the guard down to clean them out," I thought aloud.

"Two vampires," Taranis reminded me. Then, his smile grew large. He disappeared for less than a minute and reappeared wearing a foul-smelling coat and a muddied face and carrying a clay vessel of strong wine. He took a few liberal gulps, allowing it to trail down his chin. "The guard shouldn't have all the fun. Let us begin with the humans and disguise my face so you, their sovereign, can sweep in." He let the sarcasm drip on the word "sovereign" for a moment, then popped to his feet and ambled lazily towards the blacksmith. His body language and costume making him unrecognizable.

While Taranis headed to the front door, I sped around the back and jumped to the open loft in which to observe from the shadows. I wouldn't interfere unless needed—Taranis could have his fun. My dear brother banged on the door and shouldered it open, spilling a little wine for effect.

"Smithy," he slurred. "I have a job for you." Then he seemed to take note of the extra men. "I didn't realize you had company." He stumbled backwards teetering and landing squarely on his backside while hoisting the wine up to prevent a spill. He laughed at his success. "See, I have not had too much to drink, observe." He grinned at the vessel of wine again, taking another swig. Then, he loudly whispered to the wine, "That barmaid was wrong. I am handsome and I can clearly drink more."

"What dost thou want?" one of the strangers asked.

Taranis staggered to his feet and practically fell on the man. He breathed on him while he spoke and held onto him to stand. "Do I know you? I think I know you."

"No. Ye do not. What do ye want?'

"Smithy, do you know him?"

The Blacksmith, Maurus Smith, trembled and tugged at his leather apron. Never had I seen this burly man appear nervous. He was a mighty oak with trunk-like arms and a thick neck. Years of pounding iron made him as strong as the metals he worked with. "Friend of a friend," he stammered.

Taranis guzzled another few gulps and offered the vessel to the man he was still hanging on. The man shoved at Taranis. Pivoting, my brother fell over, dragging the man with him to the ground while expertly guiding his head to the anvil. The clunk of the blow to the head boomed in the crackling hot workshop. Taranis then toppled on top of him. But I hadn't missed the movement. The second the man's head struck the anvil, Taranis had snapped the man's neck with a simple turn of the wrist.

Practically falling on him again, Taranis shook him. "Are you all right? Master, I did not mean to jostle you so." He took note of the unspilt wine and smiled at the vessel again. "Ha! There you are." Then took another greedy gulp like it was a lover he'd been parted from for a long while.

One of the two other men started slowly closing in. "Richard, stop mucking about. Get up."

The third spoke to Maurus. "Finish it, Smithy."

With reluctance, the blacksmith began working again, but it was not at his usual pace. He was stalling.

I wondered what he was making for them. Taranis sloshed his bottle, drawing attention. "Now that me thinking." He swayed and shook his head. "I thinks I don't know you."

The third man became angry. "Shut ye mouth." He was obviously the leader, and Taranis had already dispatched the enforcer. I was tempted to join in, but it was readily apparent that Taranis was both having a good time and uncovering something larger than I had originally thought.

My brother staggered a few more steps until he was nose-to-nose with the leader, appearing like he had something important to say. But instead, belched in the man's face. With faux sincerity, he apologized and threw his arm around leader's shoulder. "You seem like you are in charge. What you having Smithy make?"

"Unhand me ye vile peasant. Ye ar—" Without any warning, his words cut off and he fell on a heap on the floor.

A suddenly sober Taranis started shedding his odorous coat, dropping it to the dirt floor. "He was the leader." Then he pointed to the first man he'd killed. "He was the muscle. That makes you the weak link."

The color drained from the remaining intruder's face as he took two hesitant steps backwards towards the rear door. It was my time to enter. I dropped from the loft silently behind the man. Two steps later, the intruder backed into me; he spun on his heel to face me, only to yelp in horror. He scurried backwards back towards Taranis, and once he had us at equal distance, he freed a *misericorde* from his belt, angling the thin blade at his own throat. It was the blade of a nobleman.

As my brother watched the intruder, I turned my attention elsewhere. "Maurus, what do they have you making?"

The blacksmith's head snapped up at his name; he had been so rapt in his work. Immediately, he took a knee. "My Lord," he choked. "They have my littl'un, Sire. I did not want to."

I believed him. I glanced at Taranis, who nodded; he believed Maurus too. "What did they have you making?" I asked.

Maurus scrambled up oddly fast for a man of his size and brought me some finely made pieces. He was a rare artist with metal. After a moment of examination, a terrible feeling settled in my gut. "They wanted five sets. I have two finished." He swallowed. "My girl?"

"I need you continue with the sounds of your work. Do you know where they are holding her?"

"My home last I saw her."

When I turned, Taranis was holding the *misericorde* in one hand and the last intruder in the other. Maurus returned to the forge and a moment later, started hammering. My brother asked, "When you are done with him, can I kill him?"

"Depends on the information he supplies," I answered. Knowing full well that Taranis would kill him the moment he wasn't useful.

"I...I have no knowledge of interest. I prithee thee, spare me."

"Then you may dispatch him," I replied, sounding bored.

"I mayhap have a morsel of information for ye."

"How many men in your ranks?" Taranis asked.

"T-Twenty."

"In the village?"

"No, four more here. Twenty at camp."

Taranis sighed. "Where is camp?" Then, shook him like he was dumping coins from a pouch. "Spit it all out."

"Two days on horse by following ye river. Downing trees and making camp."

I stepped in. "That sounds like more than a camp. Two days is still within my territory. Is the Duke being naughty?"

"I did not mention the Duke, prithee sir." The distinct smell of urine filled the air. I clenched my teeth in distaste.

I held up the set metal parts knowing exactly what they were —the mechanisms for siege weapons. From the heft of this, this could launch a spear large enough to carry away a full-grown man in battle gear. "How many ballista do you have?"

His mouth went slack and sweat beaded on his forehead as he debated with himself.

"My patience has grown thin." I stepped towards him, and he tried to jump back, but Taranis simply lifted him off of the ground with one arm.

"Four heavy and seven light. But only three function. We were to build a fort and send men to blacksmiths for the last of the parts. Then…" his voice trailed.

"You have almost earned your life. Continue," I ordered.

"We draw out the Prince from this castle. Take it. Once this castle is secure. We take the castle two days west. Then, nothing stands in our way. Our land will go to the sea."

Taranis whispered in his ear, "Except none of your men will survive the night."

I nodded at my brother, "Release him outside."

Taranis disappeared through the door and returned a few minutes later looking well fed. "The Duke's men taste terrible," he muttered under earshot of Maurus.

"My kingdom is the gateway to Mother's and then yours."

Maurus nervously glanced at us, but continued working. The invading party had to be close enough to hear the hammering. In addition to the blacksmith's home that left the physician and the Inn. Closing my eyes, I wished this were only Watchers or the *Raubritter* as we originally mused. *Why had my mother targeted those specific places?*

Once my carriage returned to the castle, the guard would be dispatched to retrieve me. Knowing that this could spook the town's unwelcome guests, we had to move with speed.

Taranis was already swinging the smelly coat back around his shoulders. Grinning, he asked, "So what is our plan? Drunken brawl? Midnight mischief? Stolen horse?"

I thought for a long moment. "Let us continue with your previous tactic. Go to Maurus's home and see if he wants to drink wine."

Taranis took a deep breath and a swig of wine, then swayed a moment and took on his alter ego. He dipped his head at the blacksmith and grinned mischievously. "I am off to invite you out drinking."

I stopped him. "Brother—"

He became serious for a fraction of a second. "Your people will be safeguarded."

I nodded in appreciation.

He stumbled out the rear door and looped around to the front of building so that it looked as if he were coming from the direction of the tavern. I slipped into the night, headed for the rear of the blacksmith's home. Most homes had small, uncovered windows just large enough that I could dive through one if needed.

Standing in the shadows, I peeked inside. The bedroom was empty. Light from a fire in the common room flickered through the doorless entry. A man paced back and forth. It smelled as though they were keeping a couple of sheep and a pig inside. That would explain the snuffling sound. I strained to hear more: a gentle sniffle of a child and the irritated sigh of a male—not the one pacing.

Taranis had reached the front door because a quiet knock was followed by a stage whisper. "Maurus," he laughed. "I have wine." He knocked again with the flat of his palm. "Maaaauuuruuus, Shhhhh." He shushed himself. He must have pushed at the door, because there was a sudden scrambling and the fire flickered.

A drunken voice: "You, sir, are not Maurus. Would you like some wine?"

"Be gone. Ye are not welcome here."

"Pfft. I am always welcome." A large thud boomed from the room. I wasn't sure if my brother shoved him or "fell" into the house. Just moments later, he whispered, "Belenus you are free to enter."

I rounded the corner into the house and found the cherubic girl, no more than four years old, nestled in my brother's arms, sobbing her thanks. He cooed to her and rubbed her back. It seemed juxtaposed to his usual position on humans. Though children were usually exempt from his distain —*maybe his machinations were more for show.*

One man lay dead on the floor, the other was coming around. I picked him up by the collar and dropped him in a chair. "Where are the other men?"

"What happened?" he asked confused. His head swiveled to view Taranis and fear fixed his features.

"Speak or I unleash him on you."

His pupils dilated in reaction. Taranis grinned malevolently over the child's shoulder, giving me a chill.

"Wounded—" was the only word that made it from his lips before I was out the door and around the backside of the physician's home. His home was larger than most. He had four rooms compared to two and a rear door. He used the back rooms for his home and the front two for doctoring.

The moment I slipped inside the backdoor, the scent of blood overwhelmed me—too much blood. Knowing I could no longer pass for human, I weaved through the dwelling at speed, coming to a crashing halt when I entered his treatment room.

On the table, lay a dead man with sucking sword slashes across the chest and bowels partially stitched. A series of bowls cluttered the table: cloth soaking in wine, a sponge in what smelled like opium and hemlock, and a one with clear water. Blood ran from the table onto the beaten earth floor—too much for a human to survive.

I circled the table to find the doctor frozen in a tragic pose, grasping his neck. I was there only long enough to see recognition, a glimpse of hope, and then the light leave his eyes. That flicker of hope held me in place until I could break free of it and the emotion that wanted to well up inside me.

Exhaling a shaky breath, I lurched forward and dropped to my knees praying that there was something I could do—knowing that I was wasting time. After a long moment, I gritted my teeth and closed his kind, green-grey eyes for the last time.

Forcing myself to still, I listened. There was no one else in his home and no sign of his wife, Melisende. No one moving outside. That only left the Inn, and I would need my brother's help. I slipped out the back and into Maurus's home and found Taranis still holding the little girl. He was pacing slowly while humming a sweet sad tune. She no longer looked frightened, and now the tears only stained my brother's shirt and not her cheeks.

"I need you," I whispered.

Surprise shone on his face for a split-second before it melted into his usual smug expression. I didn't think he was surprised that I needed his help, but that I so plainly admitted it. To acknowledge such things aloud often meant vulnerability—and therefore death in our world.

"We'll give her back to your Smithy and have him keep hammering?" Taranis said with question.

I nodded. "One left, and he has Melisende."

Taranis' face went blank as he strode past me towards the Smith. Once we dropped the girl off and informed Maurus that he needed to hammer to save Melisende, he readily helped. He held his girl in one arm and the hammer in the other. The clank was the heartbeat to which we walked.

After we had made our way into the forest and circled around to observe the back side of the Inn, my brother grabbed my arm. "Do you have a plan?"

I exhaled. "Other than to kill the man holding Melisende?"

"Yes."

Hooding my eyes with my hand, I pressed at my temples, attempting to clear my head. I should've fed like Taranis had. "She has aged since you have seen her. Her daughter's death…" I swallowed.

Taranis opened his mouth and shut it. He didn't approve in getting attached to humans, but he had an affection for Melisende. She could stop even someone as formidable as my brother in his tracks. Finally, he spoke, "That old crone is far too stubborn to die at the hand of a coward."

I flashed a brittle smile. *Cowards worry me more than the brave— when they know all hope is lost, they lash out and destroy things.*

The moment we were ready to enter the Inn, a carriage slowed to a halt. I didn't recognize the markings. Two horsemen accompanied the visitors.

"Go or wait?" Taranis asked.

"Wait. Let us see if they are involved."

The coachman started unloading bags at an agonizingly slow pace. It didn't appear that they were with the agitators. So, I took a knee to rest until they were out of the way. Curiosity pricked at me. I cocked my head to the side and asked, "Why do you like Melisende?"

"Like is a strong word, Brother."

I took a moment to look over my shoulder at my brother. He was keeping his face smooth of emotions. "You find her intriguing then?"

"She surprises me." He paused, gathering his words. "We were alone for the first time, and she said, 'I see you are the crooked twin.' I choked a laugh and begged an explanation. She spoke of a strange man who'd come from across the sea who had regaled her many stories of creation and the hearts of men. He'd been kidnaped by raiders and kept alive because of his magic and healing powers. She said there are always truths in legends and though she knew that we weren't the twins from her strange friends' legends, but his stories had reminded her of legend from her childhood. She'd stared at me for a long while without a word—very few humans can handle that sort of penetrating silence."

He scoured his face with his hands and after a long moment, continued. "The legend foretold of twins who would overthrow their parents. It is said that one would follow the narrow path and the other the wide path. It was foretold that if both took the narrow, more difficult path, it would bring death to the parents and usher in a new age."

"We haven't had a father for centuries," I replied.

"We still have one," Taranis countered.

"Do you really believe that legend is about us?"

A long, steady sigh hissed between his teeth. "No. I…"

Pottery breaking drew our attention and halted the conversation. I closed my eyes and listened. "I'm going to get her."

"Some cowards kill as quickly as you move," Taranis warned, echoing my own thoughts from earlier. "The Duke's men…"

But the beat of Maurus' anvil was now my war drum. I flashed across the street and through the Inn, stopping on the landing to the second floor. The smell of blood hit me before the arrow pierced my side. In surprise, I staggered to the side when I was hit by two more. I knew two things at that moment: the blood was Melisende's and there was more than one man left.

In the blink of an eye, I charged the man at the end of the hall, breaking him as I launched him through the murky window of the second story only to hear a distant thud in the nearby trees. When I glanced down, a wagon with wheels wrapped in cloth was hidden behind the Inn. *The other carriage may have been a diversion to hide the sound.* It could hold roughly six men and a driver, plus the four from the other carriage.

Feeling blood loss, I removed the two arrows I could reach so I would heal and kept them in hand. Turning on heel, I sped down the hall, jumping over the stairway to the first floor, landing square on top of the intruder who had shot me in the back. He wheezed and tried to reach his short sword, but he didn't live long enough to reach it.

"A few more left then," Taranis commented from behind me.

Swiveling, he and the pile of four bodies in front of him came into view.

"Small wagon out back. I'd conjecture five more." When my brother's eyes lingered on me a little too long, I stepped off of the man I was still standing atop and picked him up to feed as I should have earlier.

My brother's hand landed on my shoulder a split second before he tore the arrow from my back. "I assumed you weren't planning to become a coat rack."

I grimaced in pain and nodded thanks. With feeding, my wounds were all but closed.

Taranis scowled and prowled to the table in the corner, flipping the heavy, timber table over with one hand. A scoundrel wearing the Duke's colors cowered in a huddled ball. There was no more pretense. No more playing. And the soldier could see it in my brother's glowing eyes.

Raising his hands in surrender. "I was forced into service. I don't want to be here."

"Tell me everything. All at once. How many. Why. All of it."

"The D-Duke," he stuttered. "A fortnight ago, sent me with letters to deliver. I tendered 'em to merchants, tanners, smithies, physicians and the like. They were sealed with a strange insignia. Then I was to leave one at me table in the inn and another on the ground near ye stables. I returned to camp after doing me duty."

"When did you return here? How many?" Taranis grabbed his shirt front and hoisted him from the ground.

"Tonight," he sputtered. "With nine others. Meeting the men who were sent yesterday. But highwaymen ambushed us on the road. We went to the physician with our wounded, but he figured out our allegiance. Me sergeant silenced 'im and sent us 'ere with the woman."

In the distance, the sound of heavy horse from the direction of the castle came into focus, too soft for human ears. The guard was on the way. Before I could turn my attention to tracking the others, I had to return upstairs, but I was dreading it. I knew the overpowering scent of blood on the landing belonged to Melisende.

Standing still and looking towards the stairs, I closed my eyes hearing and smelling. Other than the sniveling next to me, there was no sound in this building—only blood.

"Go to her. I'll finish this."

I startled at my brother's voice and was immediately filled with dismay and didn't want to go.

"Go."

Flashing to the second floor, I followed my nose and pushed the third door on the right open. Melisende lay face down on the floor in a pool of blood and the room looked as if had been ravaged by a storm. I dropped to my knees next to her and gently rolled her over. The fatal wound had been inflicted well before we had saved Maurus' daughter.

My chest constricted in grief as I pulled her onto my lap, hating that she had died alone, when a gurgle came from her throat and she gasped awake. Hope surged and then plummeted immediately. There was no saving her from this type of wound. It was never within my power.

Her eyes sprang open and she struggled for a brief moment and froze. She stared at me through her mostly blind eyes and felt for my hand. She pulled it to her face and breathed in my scent, then cupped my hand to her cheek.

"My sweet boy," she murmured.

"Mama," I choked. Amée looked so much like her mother.

The horror that had held her face before melted into a tired smile. "Don't fret. I go to see Amée. I would have loved to have seen grandbabies, but she was too good for this world. As are you."

I made a strangled sound. "I'm not what you think, Mama."

"You have never fooled me."

"I miss her," I admitted in a foolish sounding whimper.

She cupped her hand over mine atop her cheek. "I will give her your lo..." Her hand slid away and her clouded eyes went blank. She had no idea that her husband would be joining them too.

Time stopped.

And I relived every moment of Amée's agonizing death in my arms again.

Then, the old injury of Amée's death mingled with the fresh loss of Melisende. She had taught me what a mother should be and by example, what a true partner in marriage should be. A rare human mentor for an ancient creature like me. Carefully, I slid her from my lap, crossing her arms over her chest and closing her lids. There would be more time for mourning, but not now. It was time to hunt.

When I stood, Taranis was in the doorway with the flowers I'd seen on the serving table downstairs. He took a knee next to her body and placed his hand on her forehead. He whispered something too soft for me to hear and placed the flowers in her hands. He returned to my side, exuding more emotion than I'd expected. "What do you need?" he asked.

"Execute the five left in town."

He smiled, "I thought you'd never ask."

Without hostages, we had no need for the restraint we'd just shown.

In mere minutes, we'd found all five and had them piled in the square when the guard arrived. The Captain dismounted and approached, his eyes wide. He bowed. "Sire. Are you harmed?"

Glancing down at my clothing I found that I was covered in Melisende's blood. I wiped at it absently as I thought. "Send men to collect the physician and his wife." I pointed, indicating their home and the inn. "Burial plots next to their daughter. Fortify the castle. The Duke is set on invasion."

I turned to leave with my brother.

"The Queen sent an envoy who arrived minutes after your empty carriage," the Captain added with hesitation.

"Send him home with news of the invasion. I need a horse."

"Two horses," Taranis amended.

The Captain immediately handed me the reigns of his horse and his Lieutenant did the same. "Do you require an escort, Sire?"

"No. Send a man to pick up the horses at the crossing."

The Captain's jaw flared. He didn't like my answer, but he would live with it.

Immediately, Taranis and I rode into the night. My plan was to take a boat at the crossing and make it to the Duke's camp tonight—not two days by carriage. There were caves to shelter in nearby, and we could figure a way back tomorrow.

My mind raced as we rode hard. My thoughts as loud as the thundering hooves. *If my Mother had reacted differently, could I have saved Amée's parents? Was there another reason she wanted my people dead? Were Watchers ever on my land?*

"This wasn't Mother's fault," Taranis said as if reading my mind. He slowed as did I to allow the horses a break.

Glancing up at the stars, I shook my head. "Mother should have known better. She believed the subterfuge, and my people are paying the price."

"She is rarely fooled."

I exhaled, trying to release the tension and stave off another wave of grief. His expression matched the one he gave me earlier when he told me of Melisende's story of the twins. *Did Mother know of this legend? Did she fear us? Is that why she only seems to love one of us at a time?*

Taranis nudged the body of my horse with his getting my attention. "What is your plan?"

"Find their camp and kill them all. No games."

Taranis nodded. "I am with you, Brother. Always."

Reassured, we continued into the night. Bringers of death.

MY SOUL'S FIRE—A POEM

Warmth like liquid fire.
Your heart song
Sets my soul ablaze.

—Robin Woods

EXCERPT FROM THE SACRIFICE
CHAPTER 1—AURORA

SPOILER ALERT: READ BOOKS 1-3 FIRST

ALI'S POINT OF VIEW

Kissing him was nothing like kissing Joshua, where I'd always felt like my body was a network of sparks leaving me breathless. With Bowen, I felt like I had an ocean raging inside me, undulating and pulling at my very core—waves of emotion colliding and collapsing on one another. Our breathing was ragged and fast. He pulled me closer, his arms enveloping me, my feet barely on the ground.

The barriers I'd so carefully built were chaotically crashing in on me. I wished I could tell him everything I was thinking. *I truly do care about you, but I have to leave. I can't be here. You're amazing, and if my heart wasn't broken, a part of it would be yours. Goodbye.*

Tears welled up in my eyes as I pulled myself away. He looked at me in an awe-struck daze, and I caressed his face again. *So beautiful.*

A warm tear tumbled down my cool skin, and I wiped it away with the back of my hand.

Bowen pushed some loose strands of hair behind my ear. "Is something wrong?"

My voice stuttered from an onslaught of emotion I had broiling under the surface. "No matter what, know I care about you, and I never wish to see you hurt."

He straightened up slightly and held my face between his hands, wiping the next tear tenderly away with his thumb. "I love you, Aleria. I always have, and I always will."

A sob escaped my lips. "D-don't say that. Please," I whimpered and looked down.

It was obvious he loved me, but hearing him say it aloud for the first time—now—I'd been so careful to keep him at a distance. Pushing past him, I locked myself in the bathroom.

He stood vigil at the door for a long while. He whispered my name and the words "I love you" again and again, as if I needed convincing of their truth. I anxiously watched the shadow of his feet reflected on the shiny marble surface beneath the door. When I finally exited, he was gone, and it was time for me to depart.

25

BOWEN: NOT YOURS

SPOILER ALERT: READ BOOKS 1-3 FIRST

Alternate Chapter 1 for *The Sacrifice*

BOWEN'S POINT OF VIEW

Dagan's words had been haunting me for the better part of a week—riding around on my shoulders, digging in their claws. *Not yours...not yours...not yours.* I managed to shove away the thought as I traversed the last staircase to my room.

After stepping inside, there was immediately an odd charge in the air. Aleria stood with her back to me on the steps near the bed. When she sensed my presence, she started slightly, then turned towards me. I couldn't help but grin at her; she had obviously been lost in thought—her lavender eyes looking wide and innocent. But when the expression on her face didn't alter, the horrible feeling I had just shaken returned. Something had changed.

"Are you well?" I asked, as disquiet slinked through my veins, making me feel unsteady on my feet—this was a sensation I hadn't experienced in decades.

I was losing her. *Not yours...not yours*, droned on in my thoughts. But every time those two simple words echoed in that thick head of mine, it only made me want to hang on more. I had been completely bewitched, and there was no going back. I was unsure how this girl had done it. Of course, my brother still pressed that I was in want of nothing more than her blood, that the allure of the Lux was an elixir that couldn't be resisted by man or monster. But it was more than that. She had intrigued and charmed me from the beginning. The strength and spark that she possessed was impossible to hide. Her moral code was utterly simple, yet she was one of the most complicated creatures I had ever met. And swath that with her ability to keep her humor in the face of adversity, how could I not succumb?

She didn't respond to my question. I almost asked her if she was well once more, but then she held out her hands, entreating me to her.

I went to her, and when she didn't drop her arms to her sides as expected, I placed my hands in hers, lightly caressing her fingers with my thumbs. It was my desire to be touching her at every waking moment—it took *all* my restraint to do otherwise. At that, it too, took all my might to refrain from telling her how I felt. She was not one to be pushed—if I did, she would surely run.

But now, *she* reached for *me*. I swallowed past the lump in my throat, not daring to hope, confusion rising in my mind as I braced myself for something. Aleria was radiating sorrow—it was palpable. She dropped my hands as we stood so close that I could feel her breath feather across the skin at my neck. *Not yours...not yours*, became my chant.

Aleria touched my face, and I suppressed the shudder of surprise that overcame me. Never once had she made such an intimate gesture. Standing still, as if she were an animal that could be easily frightened off, I allowed her to run her fingertips over my cheeks, brow, nose, and lips not once yielding a reaction. Afterwards, she held my face between her palms. I still didn't know what to think; all I felt was sadness and confusion pulsing from her.

At the moment I expected her to pull away and retreat from me, she did the last thing I anticipated: she closed the gap between us and pressed her lips to mine. There was no quashing my surprise this time. A gasp escaped me as I eased into the softness of her kiss.

She pressed closer, drawing me in. I still felt as if she might run and tentatively put my hands on her hips to test. In response, she ran her hands up my arms and around my neck, and it was then that I felt the emotion I had longed to feel in her break free.

Love, yearning, and desire raged inside her as she ceased being gentle. Her hands twisted in my hair and she tugged me even closer still. When I felt the tip of her tongue brush my upper lip, I gasped again. No longer capable of restraint, I ran my hands up her back, catching my fingers on the soft fabric of her shirt. I didn't pull my hand away but let it slide against the bare skin atop her spine. Pressing my palm flat against her back, I kissed her harder, my breath ragged.

She tasted like the embodiment of all my desires. Like joy was possible in this wretched world. It was as if her innocence and purity could revive the shadow that had settled over my soul. I moaned softly and wanted nothing more than to lift her and carry her the remaining distance to my bed. But that couldn't be, not without defying my mother—and more importantly, without violating Aleria's ideals. She was old-fashioned, and I loved her even more for it; values like hers had died out with people generations ago.

As her emotions stormed, confusion set in once more. She pulled back and wiped at the tears that had spilled down her cheeks.

I gazed at her, but there were no words that could contain what I felt.

She ran her fingers down the side of my face and noticed the crimson that colored her hand. Her voice was choked with tears. "There's blood in my tears."

I tucked a lock of hair behind her ear as I responded. "Is something wrong?"

There seemed to be some emotional struggle, then she captured my face between her hands. "No matter what, know I care about you, and I would never wish to see you hurt."

I bit my lip to silence myself. *No...no...no!!* erupted in my head. These words were not declarations of love; they were goodbye. Squaring my shoulders, I drew in a breath. I was out of time. I had to tell her how I felt; she was slipping through my fingers even still. I needed her to *hear* the words, though it was no secret.

I leaned in and rubbed a tear from her cheek with my thumb. "I love you, Aleria. I always have, and I always will."

She made an uneven sobbing sound as she sputtered. "D-don't say that. Please," she whimpered and looked away from me. She might as well have staked me. I tried to pull her into my arms, but she pushed past me, sprinting into the bathroom.

I stood helpless outside the door and whispered, "Aleria, I love you," again and again, hoping that she would hear my pleadings. Leaning my forehead against the door, bracing myself with the frame as I waited.

Not yours reverberated like a drum. *Not yours.*

BREATHLESS—A POEM

Breathless confessions,
Joys like brilliant sunshine.
Unfurling feeling,
Warm brushes of softest lips.
True love revealed.

—Robin Woods

EXCERPTS FROM THE FALLEN:
PART TWO

SPOILER ALERT: READ BOOKS 1-5 FIRST

Excerpts from Chapter 29—I Am Not Right

In the French Coven

ALERIA

...Gabriel cleared his throat. "We received some intel recently and sent Raphael to investigate. He reported that nothing was out of order, but that his gut told him something was wrong. So he stayed."

"Where?" I asked.

"California."

The blood in my veins crystalized. My heart stopped beating. The world stopped spinning. All existence splintered into a million irreparable pieces. There was only one reason Gabriel would...

"Ali—"

"Don't say it," I moaned.

"Batariel sent two of them into your parents' home—"

"Please. Don't say it." I could feel Joshua's emotion layered with my own.

"They split up once they entered the house—"

"Gabriel," I pleaded, my voice rising. "I did everything right. I left. I let them think I was dead. I stayed out of their lives to protect them. I did everything right. It's not fair!"

"Raphael saved your brother."

Tears burst from my eyes. "Cameron is okay?"

"Yes," he paused. "He saw everything, though. He knows our world exists. Raphael managed to kill the Fallen, and then called cleaners. As far as the world knows, your entire family perished in a fire."

A sob lodged in my throat, and my mind started to sprint through the possibilities. I tamped down the loss of my parents and focused on Cameron. If I didn't, I was afraid I might literally fracture. Could grief break bone and collapse bodies? It felt like it could.

I stood and started pacing back and forth, shaking out my hands.

"Where is Cameron now?" Joshua asked.

"He was smuggled into Geneva. Raphael is getting papers for him there. It will take another two days. He is awaiting my orders."

My voice was weak. "I want him with me, but if he comes here...he will end up..."

Bowen finished, "Being turned or becoming a familiar."

"I can take him...train him. He's my family too," Joshua offered...

GABRIEL

I did not sense Belenus, but I smelled him.

"You are leaving her alone?" I asked.

"She will be asleep for a few hours," answered he.

I closed my eyes again, but when I did not hear the door open, I opened them again. He was standing with his hand on the knob and his head pressed against a panel of the door.

"May I help you with something?" I asked.

He rolled his head to the side. "Joshua threw her away like that to save her family?"

"Yes." I noted to never underestimate vampire intelligence.

He did not reply, but left the room. I caught a glimpse of Morpheus just outside the door. I wondered what he would do with that information.

ALERIA

Hours passed. I sat on a stone bench of the veranda, a statue myself. I searched the ocean, the stars, and the night—for some sort of answer. I was praying for clarity and wishing for a light to shine down from heaven and a list of instructions to magically appear in front of me.

...When dawn was no more than an hour away, I broke from my position and headed back to my room...

I crawled onto the bed and sat cross-legged, facing Bowen. I pulled one of his hands onto my knee and laced my fingers through his.

"Are you leaving to be with your brother?" he asked...

BOWEN: FOREVER

SPOILER ALERT: READ BOOKS 1-5 FIRST

Alternate Chapter 29 of *The Fallen: Part Two*

BOWEN'S POINT OF VIEW

Handing Gabriel a cell phone, I spoke while moving towards Aleria's room. "I'll leave you to make the call."

"Wait," Gabriel beckoned.

I halted, dread weighing my body. I was tempted to ignore his request, but there was an uncharacteristic hitch in the Slayer's voice.

"I want you prepared for her reaction."

I uttered a curse that had been out of fashion for centuries and sat across from him.

Gabriel clutched the phone in his hand, the commendable control on his emotions slipping. "Batariel knew he had lost; he sent some of his people to eliminate Ali's family."

This was not what I had been expecting, though I wasn't sure what I had actually been anticipating from him. "Was the assassin successful?"

"I sent a Slayer, Raphael, to intercept. He rescued her brother, but both of her parents lost their lives." Raphael wasn't just any Slayer. He was one of the Angels of the Four Corners, like Gabriel. Even I knew that this wasn't ordinary. Gabriel had sent one of the best of his kind.

Empathy overwhelmed me in a violent wave until I was able to subdue it. I released a shaky breath, rose to my feet, then nodded at Gabriel. "Thank you for telling me."

"She is going to need you. She sacrificed every aspiration she had in order to shield them."

"I know," was the only reply I could conjure.

"One more thing." He paused. "She will want to retreat from you. She hates burdening other people; she thinks it is selfish. Help her anyway."

I nodded and began to go to her room, but before I could step away from the couch, Aleria opened her door. She was deathly pale, and it made me want to sweep her into my arms and carry her away.

A brave expression replaced the glimmer of terror I saw in her eyes as she took her place next to me on the couch. There was nothing I could do to prevent the loss that was about to befall her. Taking her hand felt inadequate, but I enfolded it in my own.

Joshua entered the room, wearing my clothes. Aleria's attention flitted to him for a moment; it was then I realized that this news would impact him too. He perched himself on the other side of Aleria. I might normally have felt jealous, but I was still reeling from the Slayer's admission.

Gabriel cleared his throat. "We received some intel recently, so I sent Raphael to investigate. He reported that nothing appeared out of order, but that his gut told him something was off. So he stayed."

"Where?" Aleria asked.

"California."

Aleria stilled, and her hand grew colder. She didn't need the Slayer to continue.

"Ali—" he began.

"Don't say it," she ordered.

"Batariel sent two of them into your parents' home—" he continued.

"Please…don't say it," she pleaded.

"They split up once they entered the house—"

"Gabriel," Aleria sputtered. "I did everything right. I left. I let them think I was dead. I stayed out of their lives to protect them. I did everything right. It's not fair!"

"Raphael saved your brother."

"Cameron is okay?" she softly confirmed.

"Yes. He saw everything, though. He knows our world exists. Raphael managed to kill the Fallen, and then called cleaners. As far as the world knows, your entire family perished in a fire."

A powerful wave of grief surged from her, and there was nothing I could do to comfort her in this moment. She dropped my hand, almost leaping from the couch, and began pacing back and forth.

"Where is Cameron now?" Joshua asked.

"He was smuggled into Geneva. Raphael is getting papers for him there. It will take another two days. He is awaiting my orders."

She sounded hopeless when she responded. "I want him with me, but if he comes here...he will end up..."

It pained me to finish her statement with, "Being turned or becoming a familiar." Her brother wouldn't be safe.

It surprised me when Joshua spoke. "I can take him...train him. He's my family too."

Closing my eyes, my nightmare became true. Asking Aleria to stay with me and not join her brother seemed the most selfish of requests. This was no place for a human boy.

Gabriel sighed. "I am sorry." He covered his eyes with his hand. "I am so sorry," he repeated under his breath. He wasn't the only one, and until now, I didn't think I understood the depth of relationship Aleria and the Slayer had. *He considered her family too.*

Aleria swayed on her feet, looking like she would collapse. I scooped her into my arms and carried her to my room, still wishing I could run with her and escape the implications of the news. I swept the door shut with my foot, blocking out all distractions.

Her brow was furrowed and her breathing rough as she twisted my shirt in her hand. I held onto her, not wanting to put her down. I kissed her hair; she tilted her head back, her pained eyes meeting mine. I kissed every angle and curve on her face. But then it was my turn to sway on my feet; the thought of losing her now that I had finally had her was unbearable.

She clung to me, burying her head into my chest—the intensity of her grief more than anyone should have to bear. Despite this, her voice was steady. "I go through things, and I think that nothing can be worse than what I have just gone through, and then it's like the universe is laughing at me and makes it worse. I don't understand. Why?"

"Give me your pain," I cooed.

She protested, "You have your own pain; you just lost people you love."

The Slayer knew her well. "Gabriel said you would do that."

"Do what?"

"Think it was selfish to rely on me. He told me not to let you get away with it."

"Damn traitor," she grumbled.

I couldn't help but laugh. She laughed with me, though as soon as she smiled, a new wave of grief overwhelmed her. I nudged her, but she wouldn't meet my eyes. "Hey," I pressed. "Give me your pain."

"I don't know how."

"Give me your pain," I whispered, finding the pulse point in her neck. Biting down, I flooded her. Then I focused on her pain, drawing it from her. It was bitter, and I knew it wouldn't last, but I took it upon myself.

Then answers that had been puzzling me suddenly became clear. Joshua had ended their relationship because Batariel had gotten to Joshua. He had done it to protect her family. It was the only explanation. When he hadn't told her, it had nothing to do with trust. He had wanted to protect her. He didn't want her to have to choose between him and her family. He would make the sacrifice and not her; it would be easier for her to hate him rather than to have to choose. It wouldn't take her long to figure it out. And when she did, it would make it easier to leave and be with her brother.

I forced myself to remain calm; I wasn't sure what it would do to me when she left. I had seen our future—been foolish enough to picture us together for centuries. I captured her face in my hands. "It is incomprehensible how much I love you."

Confusion threatened to cloud her eyes for a moment, but she was still under the influence of my bite, and I watched as the thoughts drifted away, replaced only by need.

She kissed me without restraint, a reckless desire emanating from her. She wrenched off her shirt and unfastened her pants. I needed her too. I ran my hands down her sides, easing her pants over her hips. She leaned back on the bed, letting me strip the last of her clothing. Then she stood again, helping me with mine.

She was almost frenzied, but I forced her to slow. This would have to last—each touch and each kiss a monument to what we could have had. Aleria pushed herself into the middle of the bed and I stopped to admire her, loving every inch of her beautiful body. Her curves made me want to consume her and give her everything in the same instant. She reached and pulled me down on top of her, her flesh singing to mine. Her lips parted as I kissed her, the soft moan I always yearned to hear escaping. But she was still rushing. And this, I would not–could not–rush. When I slowed once more, she responded, arching beneath me.

"I love you," she murmured, as I trailed my tongue down her neck.

Worshiping, I kissed my way down her body. There was no doubt she loved me, and this made it even more excruciating. Pressing my ear to her heart, I listened to the strong rhythm, the sound of it more beautiful than a symphony. She wrapped her legs around me, her hands in my hair.

Would I fight for her or let her go?

Answers would have to come later. For the moment, I ignored my nagging questions and lost myself in the sensation of being with her.

Aleria had finally fallen into a deep slumber and looked at peace. She would be out for quite some time. But I was in hell. I grabbed my phone from my pants on the floor and sent a text to Morpheus. "I need you." It sounded desperate and weak, but I didn't care.

"Where?"

"My room. Stay outside."

"On my way."

I cloaked my presence and slipped into the main room, intending to wait in the hall for Morpheus.

The Slayer spoke without opening his eyes. "You are leaving her alone?" he asked, peeking at me.

"She will be asleep for a few hours."

He closed his eyes, seemingly satisfied.

I was about to leave; I could sense Morpheus was already outside, but I had to confirm my suspicions. I needed to hear it, even though I knew I was correct.

"May I help you with something?" Gabriel asked.

"Joshua threw her away like that to save her family?"

"Yes."

He made no pretense—I appreciated that. I nodded and slid outside the door.

Morpheus looked at me quizzically. I wasn't sure what he saw, but he took my elbow and guided me away from my rooms. It probably wasn't wise being seen this way by the guard, but I quickly let go of my aversions.

We made our way to the anteroom behind the throne. This room had always been my refuge, but recently it had become Aleria's. I tried not to think about what we had done in here several days ago, so I compartmentalized the thought.

I sank into a chair and wrapped my fingers around the arms, pressing the metal embellishments with my fingertips. I wasn't sure how long we had been siting there in silence before Morpheus startled me by speaking.

"Unless you would like me to delve into that mind of yours, I would start talking. I'm not actually a mind reader."

"Aleria's parents were murdered."

Morpheus frowned. I knew he cared more for her than he would admit. "How is she taking it?"

"As well as could be expected."

"And this has upset you?"

"The Watchers managed to save her brother."

There was a long pause. "And this is bad?"

"Would you bring a human boy that you cared about to this place?"

"Of course not. Let the Watchers take care of the boy." There was another long pause. "You think she will leave to be with her brother."

"Yes."

"Why do you think she will leave?"

"He is her family. You have seen the lengths she will go to for people she considers family."

"Belenus." He waited until I met his eyes. "You are her family now too."

"Not blood."

"Yes, blood. You exchanged it in your vows, and I assume in your bed. You are acting like a brooding schoolboy."

"He's her brother." I couldn't see past it.

"She won't leave."

"And if she says she is?"

Morpheus frowned at me. "Then you let her go."

Feeling no better, Morpheus urged me back to the room. But when I reached the top of the staircase, I caught a glimpse of Aleria on the veranda facing the ocean. The wind was whipping her hair around her in a thrashing motion, unfazed she sat as still as the stones that made up this castle.

I wanted to go to her, but the set of her shoulders told me she needed to be alone. So I stood and watched her until I couldn't bear it. Perhaps I *was* being a schoolboy. I leisurely walked back to the suite, though I did stop to check on her again at the next bank of windows. She still hadn't moved, though I did notice guards standing in the darkest of the shadows. It eased my mind.

It was becoming necessary to feed, so I changed course and headed back downstairs. When I arrived at the door to the familiars' wing, I realized that I hadn't fed in here in years. It certainly wasn't common for royals to frequent. I pushed through the door, only to be met by Celeste. Stopping short, I glanced behind me at the door. *Was I really about to bolt from the room like a caught child? Schoolboy, indeed.*

With a tight smile, I nodded at her. "Celeste."

She seemed to smolder as she stood there, her fingers running across the low neckline of her white dress. With wanton eyes, she bowed instead of curtseying, making sure I could see more than I should have. "How may I be of service, Your Majesty? May I see you to one of the rooms?"

I found myself wishing that Morpheus had ordered Batariel to take over a year of her memory, not just the attack. Almost immediately, I regretted the thought.

"One of your ladies in the main parlor is fine."

"But, Your Highness?"

"Celeste." Her name came out a bark.

"Of course, sire." She curtseyed and slowly walked from the foyer, not looking as hurt as I would have expected—but rather angry.

I fed and tried to shake the distaste I had about the situation with Celeste. For her to react in that manner, her ambition was greater than I had thought. *She may have to be dealt with.* I cringed at the thought.

Taking two steps at a time, I went back upstairs, stopping at the windows to see if Aleria was outside. She was, and I didn't think she had moved since I had last seen her. Reaching out through our bond, I tried to sense what she was feeling, but there was nothing. I wished that I had some sense of what her decision might be. As it was, I felt like a man on the gallows praying for a reprieve. Despair seized me once again, and with no other place to go, I continued back to the Royal Suite.

Cadeyn was outside, and with the slightest of bows, opened to door for me. I was surprised to see him here, but he didn't like having the Slayer on site. He had made that very clear. Nine years ago, Gabriel had killed his closest friend, Breton. Though, I knew Gabriel had done so because Breton had killed his sister. I had never cared for Breton. He had liked to wound creatures, just to watch them bleed. I shook off the thoughts of Breton and entered with only a nod to Cadeyn.

Gabriel, Joshua, and the human Watcher were all in the sitting area, the room absolutely silent. Joining them, I took a chair. My thoughts drifted to the past. If my brother hadn't been on a binge of recklessness in Philadelphia that night, I wondered if I would have ever met Aleria. The pain of the loss of my brother began to rise, so I decided distraction would be best. Maybe it was more than a distraction; part of me felt that Joshua had a right to know more about his origin.

I looked at Joshua. "I saw you the night you were turned."

His brow furrowed, and he swallowed hard. "You were the one who pulled Tyran out?"

I nodded. "We had been fighting that night. He wanted me to go back to France with him, but I had refused. In typical fashion, he lashed out with a trail of bodies. I had tracked him to the bar, but thought I had missed him and went to the roof. Both of you were on the opposite side of the building. When I crossed to that side, I witnessed him swat you across the alley. With the blow to your head, I was sure you were dead. After deliberating my approach to my brother for a moment, I was about to drop in, but you managed to get to your feet. When he charged at you, and you succeeded in staking him, I stood dumbfounded. He had never fallen for so simple a trick.

"I dropped into the alley and checked on the girl first. She was alive, so I closed the bite wound in her neck to stop the bleeding and placed her just inside the back door where she would be found more quickly. Then, I pulled the stake from my brother and jumped to the roof with him. He immediately started to stir. I remember grabbing onto his lapels and hissing, 'You are an idiot!' then breaking his neck, so he wouldn't run off again."

"You didn't leave then?" Joshua asked.

I shook my head. "No. At a glance, your wounds were fatal, and I didn't want you to suffer. I was going to end you. But then I could smell it from the rooftop: you were going to turn. I was going to make my brother take charge of his progeny. Just as I was about to drop back in, the bearded Watcher came running into the alley."

"Sebastian."

"Yes. I tracked him from the top of the roofs. I was going to take you from him, but when he got out onto the street, he was met by two Slayers. I recognized you," I said as I nodded to Gabriel. "And Michael. I wasn't about to take on two of the most legendary Slayers by myself over a boy I wasn't sure was going to survive the change. So, I gathered my brother and saved my fight for another day."

Joshua appeared confused. "I thought…"

When he didn't continue, I guessed. "That you had been abandoned?"

"Something like that."

"My brother and I parted ways for several months after that night. I found him when the news was tittering with headlines about a serial killer. Somehow, I knew it was him. If I hadn't…" *If I hadn't, Aleria would have died the night my brother had found her.*

The room was quiet for a long while, but it was apparent that the Slayer was mulling on something.

"What is it, Gabriel? I may not be this forthcoming when next we meet," I said.

"When Breton murdered my sister. Who was with him?"

"Why do you think he wasn't alone?"

"Was it you?"

I held up my hands in surrender. "I went to America in 1775. Wars are good for vampires. I didn't return until my darling mother retrieved me in California."

"Please."

"A vampire by the name of Lazar, from what I understand, but he must have gone to ground. I haven't heard about him for years."

Gabriel looked at Joshua, but Joshua's face was blank. Whatever it was, Joshua didn't remember. I leaned back further in my seat, reading them.

"When did you kill him?" I asked.

"Your mother and brother used him to harvest what they had needed from Ali."

I had wondered how they had gotten to her. "Then I'm glad he's dead."

That was the end of our discussion.

Aleria entered over an hour later, her expression unreadable. When she wouldn't look at me, I knew it was over. She was going to leave. She hesitated before she said anything, but she finally met my eyes. "May I speak with Gabriel alone?"

I went to her and brushed a kiss across her forehead, then retreated to my room. I thought I had been in hell before, but this was worse. I could hear murmuring in the other room, they were talking purposefully low.

I started a fire, turned off the lights, and sat leaning against the headboard. It was an hour before she came to my room. I tried to smile, though couldn't manage more than a shadow of a grin.

She crawled onto the bed and sat cross-legged in front of me. Then she took my hand, entwining her fingers with mine, and propped it on her knee.

"Are you leaving to be with your brother?"

Aleria pinned her brows together. "Is that why every kiss has felt like a good-bye since yesterday?"

I swallowed, unable to muster an answer.

She kissed the back of my hand, saying, "I'm not going anywhere—I'm not leaving you—ever."

My hopes dared to soar for a moment, but I controlled the feeling.

Before speaking, she took a deep breath. "I spent all night trying to figure out what is best for my brother. I am not right for my brother right now, but Gabriel is. He has agreed to take him on like he did me. Joshua is the family he will need; he will also help with training. When Cameron finds out that I am alive, he is going to be angry, but if he knows our world, I think he will understand." She smiled. "In a few months, maybe I can see him. Even if it is limited, I can still be part of his life."

"And Joshua?"

She crawled onto my lap, straddling me. "What he did was for a good reason, but it doesn't change my decision." As she leaned forward and kissed me, my hand moved to her waist.

"Aleria," I murmured, her name never sounding sweeter.

Her brow furrowed. "I'm going to cry very soon, and it's going to be ugly. I can feel it coming. I lost my parents. But right now, I need to be selfish. I need your hands on me. I need to know that we are okay—that I have one stable thing in my life."

The last doubt I had ever had was suddenly washed away. I had been holding back a small piece of myself until this moment. She had chosen me of her own free will. It wasn't to save her own life or the life of someone else. And she had never, even for a moment, desired to be on the throne—I had heard the truth in her heartbeat. *She was mine, and I was hers.* I pushed her onto her back, settling on top of her, and propped on my elbows.

"You woke a part of me that had been asleep for centuries. You are the blood in my veins. I lived before, but now I am alive. You have given a husk a soul."

"I will love you until I am nothing but ash," she repeated from our vows.

I kissed her then, like it was my last—but knowing it was *forever*.

ARTWORK

ARTWORK FOREWORD

The following paintings were either referred to in the series or served as inspiration.

2

A MERMAID BY WATERHOUSE

A Mermaid (1900) by John William Waterhouse.

This painting was the inspiration for the development of Ethan's painting in *Allure*. I changed the scene, but the colors and tone were based on this painting.

A romanticized portraiture of a mermaid, in amazing detail adorned the canvas. She was hidden behind some rocks, watching a boy, no, a man. His expression was obscured because he sat with elbows on his knees and hands over his face as if to hide some look of anguish. Sunlight warmed his dark wavy hair…

Then I focused on the mermaid; her long dark hair hung in a way such that it hid her half nude body. She looked as if she were about to reveal her existence to him. The scales on her lower half looked iridescent in blues and purples and greens. I don't know if I had ever seen anything so beautiful. [*Allure*, Chapter 10]

HERO & LEANDER BY WILLIAM

Hero & Leander (1828) by Etty William is a poem discussed in *Allure*. Rosemond fears that she will be the cause of her beloved's death, like Hero was the reason Leander died.

This painting captures some the emotional turmoil of the situation. [*Allure*, Chapter 12]

MIRANDA—THE TEMPEST BY WATERHOUSE

Miranda—The Tempest (1916) by John William Waterhouse was inspired by the play by William Shakespeare.

While studying, Aleria wonders if *The Tempest* would have turned out differently if Caliban had been beautiful.

Caliban is ugly on the outside, yet he has more moving and beautiful speeches than most of the other characters.

Juxtaposing that, Tyran is beautiful, but he is broken and ugly inside. It isn't until later books, that we see he is far more complex (and maybe not entirely a monster like Caliban appears to be).

Joshua and Aleria also take their codenames for each other from this play—Miranda and Ferdinand the young lovers. [*The Unintended*, Chapter 2]

5

ANGEL MICHAEL BINDING SATAN BY BLAKE

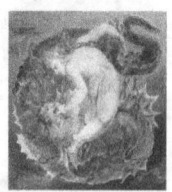

Angel Michael Binding Satan (1805) by William Blake.

A tiny, compact woman [Chloe], inked seemingly everywhere save her pixie-like face, looked up. She had abundant hair with intense purple streaks that fanned out in an amazing display; it swayed like feathers when she stood. Before she could say anything, Gabriel made a couple of signs meaning "stop" and "silence."

She nodded and, without speaking, lightly walked to a William Blake painting in the corner of the room. I recognized it as the *Michael Binding Satan* that had been in my school textbook last year. It was creepy, like most of Blake's paintings. I shuddered. She pulled the thick, black frame away from the wall and stuck her hand behind it. Then she drew out some keys and tossed them to Gabriel. He snatched them out of the air without so much as a jingle. *How does he do stuff like that?* [*The Nexus*, Chapter 4]

DAYBREAK BY PARRISH

Daybreak (1922) by Maxfield Parrish is referred to in *The Nexus*. After Aleria is saved from the dungeon, she soaks in Bowen's tub and is startled by the beauty of his rooms. The murals in the bathroom remind her of this famous piece of artwork (that was the most sold print in the 1900s).

I didn't care how hot the tub was; I plunked myself inside. The bubbles tickled my chin as I leaned my head back and listened to the bubbles popping and the sound of my own breathing.

The ceiling was painted with clouds and a sunrise above the door, gold filigree at its borders. A painted tree branched out, extending from the edge of the gold borders of the sky, making me feel like I was outdoors. Even the bathroom had pillars, and there was a mass of highly polished marble everywhere in varying tones of beige. It felt like I was in the Maxfield Parrish painting *Daybreak*. [*The Nexus*, Chapter 28]

OPHELIA BY MALLAIS

Ophelia (1851) by John Everett Millais is beautiful and haunting painting. At one point, Ali feels like a pawn in a political storm and feels as helpless as Ophelia.

He vanished, followed by the sound of water. The hotel didn't get very many channels, so I settled on *Hamlet.*

The wheels in my brain were spinning. Some elements of *Hamlet* struck me as I watched. I already knew the play, so there was nothing I hadn't seen before, but this time, some of Hamlet's characterization reminded me of Bowen. His feelings of loss and betrayal...not knowing who to trust... being disconnected from his own world. And for the first time, I felt like I understood Ophelia. I'd never been able to connect with her. I'd always written her off as weak.

"It's such a waste."

"What?"

"All those people didn't need to die." He watched as they carried in Ophelia's body.

"There has to be death in a tragedy."

"Guess I'm not a fan of tragedy." [*The Nexus*, Chapter 22]

BOOKS IN THE WATCHER SERIES

Fiction Books

Allure: A Watcher Series Prequel

The Unintended: Book One

The Nexus: Book Two

The Sacrifice: Book Three

The Fallen: Part One: Book Four

The Fallen: Part Two: Book Five

Light & Shadow: Shorts & Extras

Thank you for reading. If you enjoyed this book, please take a moment to write a review. It is the best way to help the authors you love. Books without reviews simply don't sell and your support is critical.

Reviews don't have to be long. Something as simple as:

I liked ___ and ___. I would recommend it to ___.

Thank you so much for your support. Blessings!

ALSO BY ROBIN WOODS

Creative & Fiction Writing Books

Prompt Me Novel: Fiction Writing Workbook & Journal

Prompt Me: Creative Writing Workbook & Journal

Prompt Me More: Workbook & Journal

Prompt Me Again: Workbook & Journal

Prompt Me Sci-Fi & Fantasy: Workbook & Journal

Prompt Me Romance: Workbook & Journal

Prompt Me Horror & Thriller: Workbook & Journal

Prompt Me Reading Log & Analysis: Workbook & Journal

Picture This: Creative Writing Photo Prompts & Inspiration

Coming in 2020:

Prompt Me Mystery & Suspense: Workbook & Journal

ABOUT THE AUTHOR

Robin Woods is a former high school and university instructor with two and a half decades of experience teaching English, literature, and writing. She earned a BA in English and an MA in education.

In addition to teaching, she has published six novels, nine creative writing books (and counting), and has multiple projects in the works.

When Ms. Woods isn't chasing her two elementary school kids around, she's spending time with her ever-patient husband, or sitting in a coffee shop wondering how vampires like their lattes.

For more information, an extended bio, free writing resources, links to social media, and free extra scenes, visit her website at www.robinwoodsfiction.com